D
BLO

May this be the only
dark blossom in your life!

♡
Neel

DARK BLOSSOM

NEEL MULLICK

RUPA

Published by
Rupa Publications India Pvt. Ltd 2019
7/16, Ansari Road, Daryaganj
New Delhi 110002

Sales centres:
Allahabad Bengaluru Chennai
Hyderabad Jaipur Kathmandu
Kolkata Mumbai

ISBN: 978-93-5333-294-5

First impression 2019

10 9 8 7 6 5 4 3 2 1

The moral right of the author has been asserted.

Printed by HT Media Ltd, Gr Noida

To
My **D***ad* *and* **M***om*
D*ream* **M***akers*

Contents

White Noise

When Sam had called to schedule a session for the first time, his anger had been palpable. I remember, because I had surprised myself by picking up on the vibe. Recognizing anger is something I have failed at in my own life.

He was the first new patient since I had restarted my counselling practice. Given the recent upheaval in my life, I had taken a hiatus of about half a year.

I opened my office door and saw a few patients waiting. Over the drone of white noise, I wondered how I would identify him.

'Sam?' I said, to no one in particular. Some of them looked up and others craned to look around. My eyes turned to the one man who hadn't budged. Now that I remember everything so clearly, it's possible it was his foot that had caught my attention—he was tapping it furiously on the carpet. His complexion was darker than his name and accent had led me to assume. He was wearing a brown plaid jacket, a grey cashmere sweater, and a lilac pencil-striped shirt. One side of his shirt's collar was crumpled under the sweater and he still had his overcoat on. A magazine lay open on his lap but his gaze was fixed elsewhere.

He was pleasant to look at but his dishevelled salt-and-pepper hair and unkempt beard gave him a dreary aura. I gambled. 'Sam?' I said in his direction, accompanied by a perfunctory wave to break his gaze. He looked up and, to my surprise, began the languorous process of peeling himself from the chair. The magazine slipped between his legs and landed on its spine.

What do you know? I thought. *He is my Sam.*

'Hello,' I offered him a handshake.

'Cynthia,' he said, wrapping his hands around mine and then just stared down from an inch or so higher. That's it. Not another word. I met his eyes with a steady smile and tried withdrawing my hand but his grip was firm and his hands were warm, somewhat of a respite for that time of the year.

He finally let go of my hand and stepped into the office. Falling on the couch, he trapped a sigh, or it could have been a grunt. He took in the meagre surroundings, his eyes briefly hovering over the small desk behind my seat and then settling to scan the bookshelves on the other side. 'You must love the architecture of the city…humph…there is a lot of it to love, I'll give you that.'

Besides the complexities and nuances of the human psyche, architecture is my other favourite subject—it gives me constancy and refuge when I need it.

I gave him a minute to settle in before asking, 'Where would you like to begin? Do you want to tell me—'

'Why don't *you* tell me?' he flashed, cutting me short.

I wasn't sure what had caused the sudden upsurge.

He looked away. 'Where would you like me to begin?' he said, after regaining his composure.

I wasn't prepared for a counter-question. I veered. 'When

we spoke earlier, you said it had been almost five months. How have you been doing?'

His eyes narrowed as they turned towards me. 'How have I been doing? I've been messed up...is how I've been doing! What do you want me to say?'

Some days I need to work hard at being patient, I reminded myself.

Given his loss, anger was a natural response. When we had spoken on the phone, one of the things he had said that had struck me was, 'I thought I was stronger... I thought I could do without answers...'

First, I have to placate Sam, I thought. 'I can see you're very angry...'

'You think?' he boomed.

I calmly called him out. 'Sam, you've come to me for help.' I rested my hand on his. 'You're going to have to work with me.'

He fidgeted, retracted his hand, but continued looking at me. His eyes finally widened enough for me to see that they were brown, bordering on hazel. I pressed home the advantage. 'Why don't you tell me everything...from the beginning?'

'From the beginning...' he echoed softly and settled his gaze on a small rip in my rug.

I waited.

He continued looking at the rip and began slowly. 'It was the day before his last birthday. It was a Friday. They had brought his friends and their parents to watch Spider-Man... the musical.'

Did he say musical? He sounded anything but.

His voice was cracking and he spoke haltingly. 'He was Will's favourite superhero,' he said, looking at me. 'He didn't

3

know his friends had bought Venom's costume—you know the black one—for him...for the Halloween party at our place the following weekend.'

There's something about that date, I thought, but my train of thoughts couldn't stop at that station long enough.

'And now he...never will.' He choked, quivered, and lowered his head into his hands. He was wearing a couple of colourful but frayed friendship bands on his right wrist—I could only assume they had been gifts from his son.

It felt like the first dip of a roller coaster. I almost plunged to hug him. It had taken some practice to drive out that innate response and be aware of such projective identification without succumbing to it. I poured him a glass of water instead.

When he looked up, he fidgeted and tried wiping his hands discreetly on the couch. He reached for the glass of water. 'He would have loved it, you know.'

His fingers found a loose thread on the armrest and began pulling at it. 'I was on a flight back home when it happened. I wish I hadn't gone... If I'm wishing...might as well wish he had been with me.' He sighed. 'When I landed and switched on my phone...I had...I don't know how many missed calls and voicemails...'

Looking back at me, he continued, 'I'm usually calm... humph!' And then, staring back at the rip, 'I must have panicked. I didn't know whether to call the number back or to hear the stream of messages. I dreaded both options...but I didn't ever imagine...' his voice trailed off.

'I guess it must have been easier to press play... so I heard the first message. It was a man's voice. He was a police officer. He said they had been in an accident. He asked me to call back immediately.'

I let myself uncross my fingers under my notebook. Sam was opening up. 'I was paralysed. My phone fell from my hands and I just stood there wondering how the bastard…I'm sorry… how could he have been so calm? Didn't he know the kind of message he was conveying?'

His brow was crunched and moist with sweat. He shifted and one of his jacket buttons popped, fell on the rug, and rolled under the couch. I don't think he noticed. I didn't bring it to his attention either—he was in no condition to handle such a calamity.

It wasn't just his clothes that had seen better days—his midsection belied a strong and muscular upper body. Sam was switching between peering into the rip and looking straight into my eyes. I felt the tear in my rug had become wider but was relieved he was talking. It's a small step but an important one.

'This kid—he handed me my phone, said something, and asked if I was okay. I wanted to thank him but couldn't get any words out. I felt trapped in the belly of the plane and was afraid to make the call at that time. I don't know what I was thinking!'

He had to take another long pause. 'I started going through the messages and they all went the same way. The officer mentioned the name of a hospital in Mount Vernon… I thought he had the wrong person… I mean how could they have gotten there? I had completely forgotten they would have been driving back home…'

'I had to sit down when I got to the terminal. Finally, I made the call. I waited…and hoped the click on the other end of the line would wake me up from the nightmare. Someone answered. "Hello. Is that Mr Seth?" I knew then that it wasn't a dream.'

Sam's breathing was shallow by that time. 'He asked me to…

confirm some details…' He cleared his throat before continuing, 'The licence plate and the make of the car. All I could think of was yes…goddammit, yes…but are they okay? I still remember his cool, professional voice—it was so annoying. He was sorry to inform me that my wife and son had been in an accident and that I needed to come to the hospital immediately. I was angry—I had already heard his seventeen identical voicemail messages. I only wanted to know if they were okay!' Sam had clenched his fist and, I was sure, was piercing his palm with his nails.

Sam was switching between recounting the tragic incident and purging his emotions. He would look away while trying to remember the details and would come up for air when it got too much. That's when he looked back at me—venting, questioning, and searching.

Sam's eyes were no more than slits, a look that was already becoming familiar. 'I was angry because, in my mind, I had asked him that question a dozen times already. He just repeated that he needed me to come to the hospital, adding a "please" that time. As if that would make me feel any better,' he said, throwing up his arms.

'No sir, you need to tell me if they're okay!' Sam punched the armrest.

Behavioural patterns of the bereaved are familiar territory—I just needed to be present. There would be an appropriate time for an empathic response and questions. *It isn't going to be an easy journey—for either of us.*

'All I got at first was silence…' Sam looked away again, his voice faltering. 'When the officer finally spoke, he…he told me that both of them had been killed in the accident.' He unclenched his fist and began sobbing.

◆

Surreal

Sam was struggling to cope with their loss—Marisa, his wife of more than fifteen years and his son William, who would have turned thirteen the day after the fateful accident. I moved the box of tissues closer to him. He took a few and mopped his eyes.

Memory of that night continued gushing like blood from a fresh wound. 'The officer...Sheriff Matthews...asked me to come to the hospital to identify the bodies. I don't think I said anything. I couldn't have. He asked me if I had anyone with me and whether I needed someone to bring me to the hospital.'

Sam turned to me, 'Why didn't he ask me if I was okay? I didn't have anyone left... I didn't need anyone else...and I was definitely not okay! I didn't know what to do, so I just sat there. I always called Marisa first...

'It felt like hours before I got into a cab. I wanted to call my parents but didn't. It all felt so unreal. What was the point of asking me to come to the hospital to identify...like...identify the bodies after telling me they had died? It was like...like... giving me false hope...after ripping everything away...'

He quaffed the rest of the water and poured himself another glass. 'I didn't even realize when I got to the hospital. I think I was a block of ice by the time I got there—I was falling and was afraid I would shatter into a million pieces. Before I knew it I had spoken to Matthews and had identified the bodies. It was done. Which was weird...as if...I had expected...or even wanted for it to last longer. He told me it seemed the car had lost control and crashed into a tree...and they had been killed on impact.

'Seemed! What did he mean by seemed?' Sam arched his shoulders and flailed his arms, missing the filled glass by a whisker. 'He said there had been "no other vehicles involved and no damage to the car, except from the crash." What the fuck had happened then? I'm sorry... It's just...'

I cut him off. 'It's okay. You needn't be sorry. It's important you get all of this out of your system.' I could sense that under the volatile exterior, there was an empathic and emotional man. In just over thirty minutes he had already broken down twice, unabashedly.

By then, Sam's finger was twirling around the loose thread on the armrest. 'I told him I'd like to go see where it had happened, but he said the site had already been cleared. Without missing a beat, he asked me for my whereabouts at the time of the accident.' Sam shrugged. 'My whereabouts! What did he mean by that? Was I under suspicion?

'I didn't have the energy to create a scene so I just said I had been on a flight back home and was coming straight from the airport. He said he was sorry for my loss and asked me to come to the police station the next day. He said they "may have more questions" for me.' His frame jerked forward, snapping the thread from the armrest.

'Questions for me! Really? My head was spinning with questions of my own—who was going to answer those?

'That's when I think I lost it. He asked me to calm down and assured me he understood what I was going through. Right! He suggested it was best if I got a good night's rest and we talked the next day. His claim that they might know more by then must have pacified me. He offered to have his colleague drive me home or to that of a close friend's. Ha! Close friend? I had just lost everything that mattered to me.

'On the way back home, my mind…it was like a Rubik's cube…questions and memories…just two colours, yet I couldn't see my way through sorting them. Why had she decided to drive herself? She hated driving. What had Will been doing in the front seat of the car? I know he was turning thirteen the next day but shouldn't we have talked about it first? I was going to bake his birthday cake in the morning…and…on Sunday… we had planned to go shopping for the party next weekend…'

He swallowed half the glass of water in one gulp. 'When I walked through our yard—I should really stop calling it ours, there is no us any more—I saw all our…dammit…all the Halloween decorations. They didn't look like decorations, just eerie reminders. All I wanted to do was raze everything to the ground.'

He took another sip. 'You know…my first, most intimate encounter with death was that of my grandfather's. He doted on me and I was very fond of him. I must have been a teenager when he passed away—and that was my first personal experience of grief. I was unsure of how to behave and remember my dad handling himself with equanimity.'

He sighed deeply. 'I've never really been afraid of growing old or of dying, you know, I believe it's a natural progression.

But Will was so young…there were so many memories I still need to…needed to make with him…' his voice broke.

I placed my palm on his hand. He didn't retract it. He looked up, like he was awakening from a bad dream. 'Are we out of time?'

We had been—a while back—but I said, 'Don't worry.' I've found that new patients need a buffer at the end of the first couple of sessions and, given the gravity of his circumstances, this turned out to be important.

'Sam,' I continued, 'any loss is a reminder of what's important in life. And what's most important is family—the people that make life worth living. Losing that is never easy. It just gets easier to cope with—in time—or so is the hope.' I smiled feebly in an attempt to reflect hope.

He looked at me as if he was letting the words percolate before deciding what to do with them. Finally, he nodded and got up. When he offered a parting handshake, it was my turn to hold his hand for a little longer.

'Thank you,' he said. 'And for listening.'

I lingered at the door for a few seconds, watching him walk away, as I always do with all my patients. I take that moment to connect with the catharsis I try to bring to their lives. They never look back, and that's what I hope for them too.

◆

In the Same Boat

I love to stroll in the city but, that day, I had to be brisk. I needed to keep the cold out and didn't want to miss the next train back home. Stepping carefully on the icy pavement, I planned the rest of my day. I still had a couple of patients to see later in the evening, giving me just enough time to prepare dinner for Lily and myself. I went through a mental checklist of the ingredients that would get us through with minimal fuss. *Teens…Aargh! What I wouldn't give for her to be all grown up? Or for me to be that age again?*

As I entered the terminal, the aroma of coffee and sugar-steeped bread wafting through the labyrinth of people took my breath away. My fondest memory—that of my father standing near a pillar almost ten metres away and whispering how much he loves me, and my wonder at being able to hear it all the way across the whispering gallery—is another reason the terminal has that effect on me.

With more than forty platforms, it's the largest station in the world. That almost three-quarters of a million people pass through it every day doesn't overshadow its incredible history. The backwards Zodiac with 2,500 stars sprawled across the ceiling, the hocus-pocus the Vanderbilts fed the world about the mural being backwards because it was meant to depict god's view of the universe, and the hole above Pisces serving as a reminder of the rocket that was housed there during the Cold War era—all add to its grandeur. And these are just parts of the opening act of the gala that is Grand Central.

Descending into New York City's deepest basement to wait for the train to roll in, I looked down at the tracks running side by side. I couldn't help but think of the parallels between Sam's life and mine. While he had lost his family to a tragic accident, I had recently lost the veneer of mine to a debilitating divorce from Connor. My own loss was more bearable than his. Moreover, it was of my own making.

Following the tracks and seeing them criss-cross in the distant darkness, I thought of the paradoxes between our lives. While he couldn't stop thinking of his family because he missed them and wanted them back, I couldn't stop thinking of Connor because I couldn't get rid of the sinister shadow he had cast over Lily and me.

I suddenly found myself in the same boat as Sam. And it was my job to keep him afloat. Only, we were rowing in opposite directions.

Settling into a window seat on the train, I thought of how a fatal crash at the turn of the nineteenth century had instigated a thirty-seven-year-old visionary to recommend the extravagant remedy of razing the existing depot to build the engineering marvel that is the Grand Central Terminal. Although I'm a staunch believer in just one life, I could see how in the passing of the old there is the birth of something new.

But not for Sam. My thoughts slipped back to him.

The loss of a loved one is like an amputation for the bereaved. Even though he may transition from anger to acceptance eventually, the phantom pain may never go away. I wanted to write some notes—all I had from our session was numbness in my index finger and thumb from holding the pen too tight.

I rummaged through my handbag for my Sam-notebook. I keep separate notebooks for each of my patients—they're pocket-sized and each one comes with its own pen. That one was pastel blue with a darker, more vibrant embossing of Antoni Gaudí's mosaic-dragon from the entrance of Park Güell in Barcelona. And it had a light-green pen nestled in a matching loop. It was distinctively Gaudí, as were most of my notebooks. He is my favourite architect, after my father of course.

Sam was stuck somewhere between denial and anger but much closer to the latter. He said he had gained weight, stopped socializing, and started smoking again. His work was his panacea but he had lost his mojo even for that—something that had never happened before. He had managed to pull himself together for the funeral, but his grief had exacerbated after the family had left.

The tussle between the past and the present—that of living through the experience and venting one's emotions—is important for moving on. There is no better substitute than mourning—the lesser he mourned, the more difficulty he would have in letting go.

Yet something about our session didn't add up. It had been a while since the tragedy, yet his memories had been very vivid, almost fresh. That's not what piqued me though—what did surprise me was how angry he had been at the start of the session and how quickly he had crumbled. I wondered if he had expressed his feelings and shared the painful memories with

13

anyone since the accident, or if our session was the first time he was talking about them. It mattered less for our therapy but more for his well-being that he had others to talk to as well about such intimate details. It was clear he needed to share and express more.

The announcement for Stamford broke my reverie. Even though it had been a somewhat tentative start with Sam, I was happy to be practising again and knew I could help.

As I tucked away the notebook, my heart went out to him and then turned to Lily. I was filled with gratitude for having her in my life. She's my pride and my passion. Even the rewards for helping my patients are a distant second to my gratification from nurturing her. She had gone through a lot but the worst was finally over—Connor had moved out and the divorce had come through.

I was almost at our doorstep as I thought—*how could I have not seen it? How could my need to preserve the façade of a family have made me so blind to such a monster?*

◆

Longing for Lily

Lily and I had just begun to nurse our lives back to health. Earlier, she had been healing well and showing signs of slowly letting me back into her life. But then—ever since her breakup with bad boy Roy—she had retreated into a shell. At first, I didn't make much of it because I thought it was transitory, but she continued to shut me out of her life and I was growing concerned. Still, I was glad he was out of her life. I knew that boy was nothing but trouble.

As I opened the door, I heard Lily. 'And I'd be happiest if I never see him again!'

Is she talking on the phone? Is someone there?

I stood there, paralysed.

I heard another voice. 'But why? He says he still loves…'

Is that her friend, Joanna?

'Don't say it! Don't say that word. I know people like him and they can't love anyone—other than themselves that is.' Lily sounded livid.

'I don't know what happened between you, but he's sorry, you know.'

It is Joanna.

'Well, good for him! He's never said that to me. And even if he did, it wouldn't matter because I'm over him.'

'Wow! That bad, huh? What did he do? Why wouldn't you—'

'Drop it, Jo! Just drop—'

And that's when I did—drop it—the mail, that is. It landed with a piercing snap. I scrunched all the way from my shoulder up.

'Cynthia? Is that you?' Of course, Lily had heard the sound.

I hated her calling me that. *Why wouldn't she call me mom like all the kids her age? I didn't want her to be that grown up either.*

'Hello girls!' I said cheerfully, hoping my eavesdropping hadn't been exposed.

Damn! I shouldn't have said girls. Now she'll know. What do I do?

'Would you help me here, please?' I attempted subterfuge but it was more out of panic.

With what? It's just mail. Shoot! She's going to see right through me.

'Uh… Ah.. Actually it's okay… I got it!' I bellowed louder and quicker than I needed to.

I heard hushed whispers and then the conversation continued in the kitchen.

Phew! All the years of studying and practising psychology—the least I should be able to enjoy are fringe benefits like eavesdropping on my daughter and getting away with it. I smiled to myself.

'Hello, Joanna,' I said, looking at her, while planting a kiss on Lily's head. I squealed and flinched as I almost impaled my eye on one of her spikes. *Now, she is a sight for sore eyes!*

'Hello!' Joanna echoed, muffling a laugh, and added 'Ms

Stalwart' with a flourish. She knew I like being called by my maiden name, especially since it had become official. *Good girl.*

Lily, my darling, on the other hand, calls me Cynthia as if she's thirty but dresses like...is it a punker...or is it just a punk? It never registered. She'd gotten into a phase—I think she referred to as punk pop—since she had fallen into the Roy Band. Yup! That's how he and his entourage referred to themselves. Every time I asked her why she couldn't just be 'pop' instead of 'punk pop', I would promptly be informed that punk was the best thing to have happened to pop since...who was it now... Michael Jackson, and would be asked to 'back off!'

Another reason I was glad Lily was hanging out with Joanna—she is a well-mannered girl and dresses like one too.

Turning towards the fridge I said, 'You staying for dinner, Joanna? I'm thinking of minestrone...'

'Hmm... I could...' Joanna mumbled.

'...and a nice roasted Brussels sprouts salad with walnuts, cranberries, and some blue cheese,' I continued.

'Uh! I could not...possibly do that, Ms Stalwart.' She stumbled over her words. 'I told my parents I'd be back home for dinner. Mom hates it when I change my plans last minute. In fact, Dad's gonna be picking me up soon.'

Lily sniggered. *Joanna is a lousy liar indeed.*

I didn't know whether to be happy that the girl didn't know how to lie or to be offended by her bid to ditch my world-famous Brussels sprouts. What I was sure of, however, was that almost anything else on the menu and her response would have been different. *Well, note to self for next time.*

I played along. 'Oh yeah? That's great—tell him to come in and say hello when he does.'

Lily pounced. 'No!' Both Joanna and I turned to stare at her.

'And exactly why is that, Your Highness?' I asked. The red of her face eclipsed the jet-black eyeshadow.

She buried her nose into her book. 'Uh-uh! I mean…sure… I don't know what I was thinking.'

'Mm…hmm…' I didn't want to make a big deal of it and embarrass her any more than she already was.

By then, I was already busy washing, peeling, and chopping. And they pretended to go back to schoolwork. I recognized what sounded like furious texting coming from Joanna's direction. I wondered if the subject of such texting was to extend my invite to her father or to convince him, at the eleventh hour, to pick her up on his way home. I was pretty sure it was the latter.

I was naught for two—first with almost being caught eavesdropping and then with Sproutsgate—but I needed to make my way back into my daughter's life. So I persisted, 'How was school?'

Lily pretended to be absorbed in her book, so Joanna offered, 'Oh! It was super. Everyone's busy preparing for senior prom. It's gonna be a magical night. Lily and I have decided to go as dates because none of the silly boys deserve us!'

I laughed. 'I couldn't agree more! Have you girls figured out what you're wearing yet?'

It was Joanna who had to swoop in to fill the silence again. 'Not me! I'm going shopping with Mom this weekend. But Lily and I were just going through her wardrobe—'

Lily looked up and glared at her. 'No we weren't!'

Why wouldn't she let me in? Why wouldn't she share such a tiny little detail with me? It's not asking for too much, is it?

Joanna objected. 'Uh! Yes we were… Why wouldn't you tell your mother? You almost decided…'

It's not like I judge her wardrobe… At least vocally I don't…

18

not too much anyway… And after all we'd been through together? I had watched out for her as best as I could have…

I'm sure Joanna went on to complete her sentence but I had already drifted. I could hear their banter in the background but I was embroiled in emotion, trying to figure out what it would take for my daughter to be my friend again. Given she had broken up with Roy, I wondered if she was still planning to travel to Europe in summer. *Perhaps I could propose travelling together for a while—it could be good for us.*

It was Lily's scream that pulled me out of my cocoon. 'Mom! Cynthia! The sprouts are burning.'

'Whoops!' I had forgotten to set the oven timer.

'Well! Nothing better than burnt Brussels sprouts for dinner, hon. They're going to have a little more character than I thought,' I said, as smoke belched from the oven.

Chuckles!

At least I got them to laugh.

I was barely done cleaning up when Joanna's phone rang and she sprung up. 'He's here!'

Before either of us could move a muscle, Lily said a quick goodbye to her friend and dashed upstairs, muttering something about needing to go to the washroom. I'm sure Joanna would have found Lily's behaviour strange too, had it not been for how happy she was about being picked up by her father. I was happy for her. *My family, on the other hand, would have to wait till its next turn—if and when that came.*

◆

Later in the evening, I spent some time delving into the *Diagnostic and Statistical Manual* to refresh my memory on what

19

it had to say on bereavement. Grief such as Sam's is extremely personal and so is one's way of coping with it. I knew from experience with a couple of other patients in the past, it could continue for up to two years. It would help to know the patterns to watch out for, to tell the difference between bereavement and mental illness. I updated my notes.

◆

Dinnertime got Lily and me back on the island—it's my favourite place at home and my favourite time of day as well. Growing up, I would sit with my parents for hours in the kitchen, especially around meal times, and we would share stories, plans, and, most memorably, laughter. A lot of it! In that moment, however, alone with my daughter, I was riddled with doubt. I wanted to talk about the things that mattered—find out if she was doing better since her father had left, how she was coping with her breakup with Roy, what her plans were for the rest of the year—but she was not letting me in. I knew that, first, I had to fight to rebuild a relationship based on confidence and trust—I had been trying my best and still failing.

I started heating up dinner. 'Have you thought about your plans for the summer? Are you still considering travelling to Europe?'

She didn't reply and continued setting the plates on the counter. I was sure she had heard me. 'Hon! I asked you a question.'

She had indeed been pretending—she had heard me fine the first time. 'Huh! Am not sure…still thinking about it.'

I saw an opening and wanted to plant my idea in her mind. 'Perhaps we could travel together for…'

She didn't let me finish. 'If I go, I'd like to go alone—or maybe I'll ask Joanna to join. It'd be nice to get away from here for a while—I sure could use some time off.'

'Oh!' I was bummed at being shut down so quickly. I forced myself to fake enthusiasm. 'That sounds like a terrific idea! Have you asked her yet?'

'No,' is all she said, amidst the clatter of cutlery.

It was getting worse but I couldn't give up. 'Do you know where you might want to go?'

'No,' she said sitting down with a grunt. 'Can we eat now, please? I'm hungry.'

I served dinner in silence and took solace in the fact that she extended me the courtesy of waiting before starting to eat.

'Plans for the weekend?' I persisted.

'Nope! None so far,' Lily said, sidling a side of a sprout that had been spared the charring into her mouth.

I toyed with the sprouts on my plate. 'Want to spend a day with me?'

'Sure. Doing what?' She bit confidently into the sprout.

'I don't know. We could go to the mall, have lunch, do some shopping…'

'Shopping…for you?' She contorted her face, presumably because of the frustration of her confidence in the sprout.

'No. For you, Lil. For your prom!'

The fork dropped on the plate. It sounded like a gunshot.

'You don't listen, do you?' she hissed. 'We just spent the entire afternoon talking about what I was going to wear, but clearly, you don't care! That meddling Joanna—she should know when to mind her own business. Argh!' She stormed away from the island and ran upstairs to her bedroom.

Burnt! That's one too many times in a day.

I must have sat there for a very long time. By the time I put the two unfinished dinners away and went to wish her goodnight, she had already fallen asleep. I could do little but look at her lovingly and hope that things would be different—better. I tucked her under the covers and kissed her before switching off the light for fear of losing the other eye too!

◆

Grief

Sam wasn't sure he wanted to continue therapy with me and said he needed some time to reconsider. I respected his decision but told him that in my professional opinion, he needed to take care of his well-being and continue to talk about his feelings with someone he trusted. He said he understood and appreciated that. I did check in on him once just to make sure he was doing all right but he didn't reply to my text.

One day, after almost a month, he texted me back to schedule our next session. I was eager to see if he was doing better. He looked heavier than before and, I could have sworn, shabbier too. He had the advantage of age on me—only just—but much of that benefit was hiding under a matted beard, dishevelled hair and an angry demeanour. His clothes were elegant but donned with abandon. It had already started thawing and was too warm for an overcoat, but he was wearing the same coat and jacket from the first session. I thought it prudent to establish how he was doing before considering telling him about the missing button. He was wearing old, worn-out sneakers with formal pants, and I was sure his socks didn't match.

At the start of most sessions I ask my patients if they have any specific issues they would like to address. I also remind them of any themes we might have left open from previous sessions. This lets them know that it is they, and not I, who are in control of the process. It also gives us the chance to review how their thoughts, behaviour, and actions may have evolved.

'Last time you needed to talk about the painful memories from the day of the accident—are there any more you'd like to unburden?' I asked.

'No,' he said. I gave him a few seconds to be sure.

It is when they don't have any specific issues on their mind or a place where they'd like to begin, that I proceed with my plan for the session. Everyone handles grief uniquely and coming to terms with it isn't exactly made easy by a society that doesn't accept or even understand it very well. I knew he had just begun the delicate process of grieving and wanted to build a case for him to continue with therapy, at least for some time. 'I know your pain must be insufferable and I understand your anger…' I didn't get a chance to finish.

'Oh, do you?' he burst out, his face turning red and pupils dilating. 'I find that difficult to believe. You have a daughter, right?' he tilted his head and arched his brows in the direction of my desk. 'But have you ever lost a child?' He paused. 'If you haven't, then there's no way you can even begin to understand.'

Déjà vu, I thought. His anger from the start of our first session flooded my memory. I assumed he had made the connection about my daughter from the few photographs of Lily and me together that adorned the desk behind me. I have discovered there is a strong, positive correlation between the time I spend in this profession and the effort I must put in to be patient. Thankfully, it is this very awareness that helps me curb reactive, emotional responses to stimuli such as my patients' outbursts.

I tried a different approach. In a softer voice, I asked, 'Why are you here, Sam?'

'Huh?' he exhaled.

I backpedalled a bit—my question had been more for rhetoric anyway. 'I'm sorry if I offended you. I didn't mean to patronize you at all.'

Clearly, it had been too soon for me to try and wrest control. He wasn't ready for it. I stayed silent.

He finally broke the silence. 'Sometimes, I want to vent but don't know what to direct it at...at other times I have this burning desire for revenge but don't know whom to exact it from.' He gasped and stiffened, except for his flaring nostrils.

He poured himself a glass of water. 'When I'm thinking more rationally—it's difficult to believe, ha! ha!—but there are times when I am...I realize I want answers. I'm trying hard but am not getting any.' He took another pause. 'Most of all... I just want them back.' His eyes welled up.

At least he has a sense of humour buried somewhere within the rubble. I let him purge his pain. My intuition told me that under the angry and sullen exterior there was a calm and self-assured man. My training told me I just had to scratch at the right places with the right intensity for that person to eventually shine through.

When he finally regained his composure, he said, 'I'm sorry...for snapping.'

Yeah! Don't let it happen again. I always imagine myself saying it out loud with a smile—the mere musing helps sustain sanity.

Even though he had expressed reluctance to continue from where we had left off in our previous session, I decided to

25

push. That is my job, after all. 'Do you want to tell me what happened when you went to the police station the next day?'

With the more direct line of questioning, he acquiesced and began slowly. 'I don't think I slept much...or at all that night. But I still remember waking up feeling...like...someone had hit me over the head with a baseball bat.'

That's natural. Living through the experience of losing a loved one is like having a concussion. Each day brings a different kind of pain. And it's difficult to predict what it might be.

'I knew I had people to call and things to get done but I also had a list of questions I wanted to write down so I could get them answered. I just wanted someone...someone else...to make it all go away. I remember feeling relief that it was the weekend and then feeling guilty about being relieved. Everything was a mess.'

Good! He's talking again. But he isn't ready for the news of the missing button just yet.

He doffed his jacket. 'I couldn't bring myself to go to the police station during the day—so they called and came over later the same evening. It was...Matthews...and another officer. They had some routine questions,' he said rolling his eyes, 'and I thought I was never going to be off the suspects' list. But I didn't have the will to fight.

'When they were finally done with their questions, I asked them to tell me what had happened. I wanted to know every detail. I wanted some answers. The sheriff said it had been a GM OnStar service agent who had called it in. The OnStar team had been automatically notified as soon as the car crashed. They had called into the car but had gotten no response—that's when they had called 911. The sheriff's demeanour was no different than from the night before and it was just as infuriating.'

26

He paused and looked into my eyes for a few seconds before continuing. 'The police had gone to the site of the crash as soon as they received the call. It had happened as they were entering Yonkers…on their way back home…right beside some park.' He knitted his brows and continued to stare.

After a pause, he started rubbing his temples. 'And then, I remember distinctly, the officers had just looked at each other—as if silently asking what they should say next. The least they could have done is prepare in advance—I mean, after all, they did have all the time in the world on their drive over to my place!'

He was back to reliving the ghastly memories and I was confident it was the catharsis he needed.

He stopped flailing his arms long enough to gulp the rest of the water. 'After a while, the sheriff spoke. He said that unfortunately that's all they could tell me at the time. It was unfortunate all right!' he said through grinding teeth. 'They hadn't found any flats, or dead animals, or signs of an accident. The other officer said something about not having "ruled out foul play". Foul play! What was it—a set for a movie?'

His arms were lying limp by his side. His palms were turned up and his right wrist displayed possibly the only colourful remnant of his family on his being.

'I wanted to know how it had happened and Matthews kept talking about the police work they had done. He told me Marisa's death had been instantaneous, but they couldn't be sure about Will. What they did know was that both of them had…' he could barely bring himself to say the words, '…suffered serious head injuries…and had been found dead on arrival.'

Sam's voice had reduced to a barely audible whimper. 'I had to stop him and ask him to tell me exactly how it had happened—what had caused the accident? How had they both died? I mean, didn't the airbags deploy? They're supposed to, right? The sheriff said that the car had driven off the embankment and had crashed head first into a tree. Apparently, they had both been dislodged by its fall and it was possible that the deploy of the airbags is what killed them…

'Then the other officer said something about reckless driving and…and it all went to hell from there. I remember screaming whether he had any evidence… Either I blacked out or everything was such a blur that, by the time I came to my senses, they were already out of the door and in their car. And I still didn't have any answers—not the ones I needed. I asked them if they would keep the investigation open and was shocked when they said, "Not unless something new turns up". And then, they were gone.'

He brought his hands together as in prayer. 'All I want to do is find the person…find someone…find some answers…'

I asked, 'And have you been able to, since?'

'Huh? What do you mean?'

'Have you called the police since then to check?'

'Check what?'

He wasn't getting it. I was tempted to help him out but I felt I already had my answer.

◆

Alone

I had to validate a hypothesis, so I changed tack. 'It's okay, I understand. Tell me, these memories and your feelings—have you been able to share these with anyone else as well?' I gave him a few seconds.

He shrugged and just shook his head. 'I talk to my parents… although it was difficult when they were here for the funeral. Both the families were here at the same time…'

'What about siblings?' I asked.

'Only child, unfortunately.'

My notes reflected my thoughts. *Only child, small family, his social support system becomes all the more vital.*

'What about friends?'

He was still wriggling. 'I have only a few friends here and most of them are from work.'

I might be on the right track here. 'Are you close to any of them?'

'Close…hmm…not from work, but I do have a few cycling buddies as well.'

Great! He cycles. It ought to be pleasant enough for cycling soon.

I should try and get him back on the bike—it'll be good for him.

'Close enough that you can talk to them about your feelings, about what you're going through?'

He smiled faintly—it was barely perceptible under his beard. 'Hmm...I guess there's John—he's a cycling buddy and my neighbour. We're close—he's a busy guy though.'

I had seen this pattern of isolation in single children from small families a few times. Besides, I knew what it was like being an only child.

Before I could share my thoughts, his shoulders slouched and he sank back in the couch. 'To be honest, I don't have many close friends here. Before moving back to the U.S.—this time for Marisa—I had lived here for quite a few years, on separate occasions actually, but had always gone back home to be with my parents. She didn't have such a great relationship with her family, so she didn't ever want to move back. And then...after Will was born...everything changed for me as well.'

Even though I had been able to discern that he was an immigrant, I couldn't be sure about his origins. His accent was pretty neutral and even his complexion wasn't much of a giveaway. What was apparent was that he had assimilated very well.

He smiled. 'I had to work hard to set up the business, but he became the centre of my universe. So really, life's just been between...' The pause was longer than usual and he ended with, '...that.'

I didn't feel strangely about the pause but did so about the entire revelation and his choice of ending with 'that'. I felt there was something amiss but had more important concerns about his well-being.

My impression of him was that of an intelligent and

introspective person. And I like to explain the reasoning behind my thoughts to my patients—if and when it's appropriate.

'The reason I asked you whether you've been able to share these feelings with others is because it's one of the most important steps in coming to terms with a deep loss. It seems to me, you might not have very many people to do that with.'

I left an opening, but he didn't take it. I wondered how his ego would react to the potential chink. He shifted and opened his mouth, as if to say something, but stopped.

I pressed on. 'And everyone needs that. I know you're coping with the loss of the most important people, but, right now, the most important person is you. You need to be taken care of—by others as well as by yourself. You're even justified in asking for such care. So that you can get through this tough time.'

I paused for a little longer. 'I want you to know that whenever you need to share or just talk, I'm only a phone call away.'

He nodded and thanked me. He seemed calmer when he left, but I knew it would come and go in waves.

I had a few minutes to reflect on our session. I could gauge Sam was grappling with many unanswered questions about the accident. Even though grief is not a linear process, he needed to get his anger out of the way before he could mourn or find the answers he was looking for. I suddenly became aware of my own sadness. Thankfully though, it wasn't being projected as anger—I didn't have much room for that in my life, especially given my situation with Lily.

I found my thoughts meandering through my cases over the years. *More people come to me for help to alleviate the stress from unfulfilled worldly desires than those who do for help to manage the spiritual pain from a loss such as Sam's. That does suggest the convoluted nature of the world we live in.* I wondered if it was just me or if some of my colleagues felt similarly. I breathed a sigh of relief as the arrival of my next patient nipped the unsettling rumination in the bud.

◆

Epiphany

The weather had become warm, in contrast to Lily's attitude and behaviour towards me. I love summer on the East Coast and nothing clears my mind better than a run by the river near my home. I had reshuffled my schedule so I could get back from the city earlier than usual and have some time for myself before seeing the evening's patients at my home office.

One sunny afternoon, after a run, I was still panting and trying to get the door open, when my cell phone rang. Keys still jingling in my fingers, I picked it up.

'Hello! Is that Mrs Jefferies?' said a chirpy feminine voice.

'No…uh…I mean, yes it is.' I replied. *I would correct her later,* I thought.

'Mrs Jefferies, this is Celia, Principal Dean's assistant. We've met before.'

It was Celia from Lily's high school.

'Of course! Hi Celia! How're you…' I stopped short. 'Is everything okay?'

'Yes! Yes! All well, but Lily got herself into a little fight today. Well…perhaps a little more than little.' She may have giggled, but I wasn't sure.

I stopped playing with the keys. Concern spilled into my voice, 'Is she okay?'

'Oh yeah! She…is fine,' Celia continued, 'but you should see the other guy!' I noticed the humour, made prominent by a snigger, but I wasn't finding it funny—any of it.

She went back to being starchy. 'Principal Dean would like to see you.'

'When?' I asked.

'Er…right now. Lily is here too. By here, I mean in detention,' she cleared her throat. She was enjoying it—too much for my liking. I wanted to give her a piece of my mind.

'I'll be right there. Thanks.' I hung up.

What could possibly have prompted her to get into a fight, and that too, today of all days? With whom? I should have asked.

◆

I was still panting when I was ushered into the principal's office.

Mr Dean struggled to stand up behind his desk. His portliness was proving to be an impediment. 'Mrs Jefferies! So nice to see you—you needn't have made it in such a dash.' He was grinning.

What is it with everybody and their cheekiness today? He was obviously taking a jibe at my appearance. I was still in my running suit and was a sweaty mess. I didn't care—the sweaty mess was about to swaddle his finely upholstered leather chair. I ignored his pun.

'It's Ms Stalwart now actually. For Lily as well,' I added for good measure. It put him in his place.

'Oh, okay. Ms Stalwart it is.' He was considerate enough to pour me a glass of water.

I gulped it down quickly.

'Care for some more?' he asked, still holding the jug in one hand.

'No, I'm good, thanks.' I had saved a smidgen. 'What did she do now? Is she okay?'

'Well, she's okay…but she got into a fight. A serious one,' he said, sitting down.

'With whom?'

'With Roy. You know, the McCallan boy?'

'Yes, I'm familiar with his work.' I was sure he must have done something to bring it upon himself. 'What did…he do?'

Mr Dean squeezed his oversized frame into the chair and brought his hands together in a steeple on the desk. 'Well… that's the thing, you know. Apparently, the poor boy didn't do anything.'

Oh please! He's anything but poor.

'It happened in the cafeteria, in front of the entire school. He was trying to talk to her and before you know it, they broke out into a scuffle. And then…'

And then what?

He leaned forward and raised his brows. 'Lily hit him with her tray, right across his forehead.'

'Oh my god!' I couldn't believe what I was hearing. *She had gotten into trouble before, but Mr Dean was right. It was never this serious.*

'Now, I'm sure it was just a mistake, but that's a dangerous one to make. I don't think he will need stitches but he was bruised very badly. His mother was here earlier and took him to the hospital.' Mr Dean shook his head and sighed.

I asked, 'Have you heard back from her yet? Is he okay?'

He must have provoked her in some way…after all, Mr Dean

mustn't know their history. Lily must stop acting out like this…
What am I going to do with her? My thoughts were running a
million miles a minute.

Before he could respond, there was a knock on the door.
First, Celia's nose peered in and then the rest of her followed.
'Lily is here,' she announced.

'Send her in, please,' Mr Dean said.

Lily came in with a look of disdain, flopped her backpack
beside the chair, and sat down heavily without making eye
contact with either one of us—as if the proceedings were an
inconvenience and she hadn't the foggiest idea as to what any
of it had to do with her.

'Well, hello to you too, Lily. Have anything to say for
yourself?' His question was met with silence.

Looking back and forth between us, he said, 'I haven't heard
from his mother yet but I'm hoping—for your sake, young
lady—that he is okay and they don't decide to press charges.'

'I didn't do anything! It was him… He was the one…' Her
pitch was as pointed as her spikes. I rested a hand on her arm,
trying to signal an alternative approach. It had the opposite
effect. Flicking my hand with her arm, she glared at me and
said, 'What? He was the one trying to pick a fight—he was
misbehaving with me and he had it coming.'

Mr Dean jumped in, in a valiant albeit unsuccessful attempt
to diffuse the situation. 'Now, now! I'm sure there was some
misunderstanding there. But even if he was trying to talk to
you, it still didn't give you any reason to…'

Lily was pushing her palms down on the armrests and had
arched her body almost out of the chair. 'But he wasn't just
trying to talk to me. He was…he was…'

Mr Dean cut her off. 'Lily. We have the entire school as

witness. You had no reason to act out the way you did. You hurt him—it's very serious, what you did. Now, if everything is okay with Roy, and I sincerely hope that it is, you must apologize…'

She half-stood up, almost ready to pounce. 'Why wouldn't you listen to me? If anyone needs to apologize, it's him! He wasn't trying to talk to me—he was hurting me. He was grabbing me.' She flung out her arm, possibly to show where.

Crash! Splash! Her arm toppled my glass and the little water left in it spilled onto the desk.

What happened next stunned Mr Dean. Lily instantaneously transformed into this apologetic, diminutive, snivelling tyke. 'Oh! I'm so sorry, sir. That wasn't meant to happen. I'm such a dimwit! Let me clean it up real quick.' She took out her Kleenex pack and feverishly racheted out the tissues to clean up the spill, all the while continuing to apologize, 'Really sorry about that, sir. I can fix it. What a retard!'

She didn't even realize that Mr Dean's desk was covered in tissue residue. It was a mess. So was she. More liquid had poured out of those beautiful, mascara-laden eyes than what had spilled out of the glass.

Mr Dean was clearly in shock, his mouth agape and eyes flitting between Lily and me. He recoiled, slid down in his chair, and was clutching both armrests. For a few seconds, I couldn't fathom why. And then a sudden epiphany brought my world crashing down.

It hit me, how many times I had seen that transition in Lily— from a livid lioness to a meek mouse—in front of Connor. But he had never registered the surprise Mr Dean just had—Connor had just taken Lily's all-too-frequent extreme transitions in his stride. The aberrance of it all hadn't ever struck me.

Oh god! How could I have been so blind? This has been staring me in the face for quite some time. Shame on me! No wonder she blames me for not having come to her rescue sooner and is so hostile towards me.

Finally, Mr Dean got up, used one hand to hold his tie in place, put the other one gently on Lily's arm, and summoned her to stop. 'Lily, my dear, it's okay. It's not a big deal. It's just a little splash of water.'

He waited for her to calm down a bit before continuing, 'Now why don't you be a good girl, go wash your face, and wait outside for us?'

Lily left obediently, still sobbing and shuddering. Her demeanour and the mascara running down her cheeks were in stark contrast to the ruggedness of her punk getup. It would have been comical, had it not been so sad.

After what seemed like an inordinately long silence, Mr Dean whispered almost conspiratorially, 'Ms Jeff...I mean Ms Stalwart... I'm not sure what to say.'

Neither do I, Mr Dean, neither do I.

He started again. 'Your daughter is such a lovely young girl—she's popular and good at academics...'

I was just staring past him. I might as well have been performing complicated astrophysical calculations as I was coming to terms with the last few years of our lives and the error of my ways. *Having been blind to Connor and to my own pain was one thing, but how could I have been so blind to what had been happening to the most important person in my life?*

He continued, 'But what I just saw is clearly not normal. I mean—is everything okay with her at home? She seems to be really struggling with something. Perhaps you should consider having her looked at...'

I clobbered the armrests while wishing for the power to

38

shoot lightning bolts from my eyes. 'How dare you? How dare you suggest there is something wrong with her? She's just a girl who's been through a lot.'

He immediately raised his hands in withdrawal. 'I'm sorry. I wasn't suggesting there is something wrong with her. Clearly, she has gone through a lot and I was just wondering if it would make sense for her to get some help in the form of counselling perhaps. You, of all people, should know that...'

'You, of all people...' Exactly what is he trying to insinuate? My invective was stifled because his comment had hit another raw nerve. I realized why Lily was so opposed to the idea of going for counselling and so antagonistic towards my profession. *After all, someone with my alleged skill set should have been able to connect the dots better...and quicker.*

My anger turned to despondency. Then, in what I'm sure was a perfect closing act to Mr Dean's day, I broke down as well.

I finally found strength enough to speak. 'It's just that she has been through a lot lately. First, with the divorce, and then, the breakup with Roy...'

From the size of his eyes, I could tell he didn't have a clue about her and Roy. *How do I tell him there's more? So much more.*

The meeting came to an end with Mr Dean guaranteeing he would do his best to smooth over the situation with the McCallans. As he walked me out with an arm around my shoulders, I was still dabbing my eyes.

◆

At Wit's End

I tried to avoid Lily's stare as I motioned for her to follow me to the parking.

She fell in tow. 'Why are...you crying?'

She doesn't miss much, I thought. I didn't know what to say. And that's what I told her.

A few minutes later, in the car, all my training told me to be quiet but the muddled mother prevailed. 'On your last day of school ever, really! What happened?' I asked.

'It's like I told you inside, Cynthia!' the lioness roared. 'Roy was rough-handling me, and I've had enough of that.'

The tarred eyes were the only remnant of her meekness a few minutes back. But I wanted details. 'Can you tell me what happened—from the beginning, please?'

She shot back. 'Why? Is this an inquisition? I already told you he was misbehaving. Isn't that enough?'

I was trying to keep calm. 'I'm just concerned about what could have possibly brought on something so serious. Why did Mr Dean keep insisting there had been no provocation?'

'Ha! Typical! But of course—you believe Mr Dean. Why would you believe me?'

I could feel her eyes burning into me. I had a new appreciation for her lack of trust. I just hoped it hadn't crossed over to resentment.

She kept going. 'This time I just stood up for myself… because no one else ever does…not even…' Something in her must have made her stop but I knew what the end of that sentence was meant to be.

I did my best to deflect her diatribe. 'Then why won't you talk to me? What happened between you and Roy? What did he do to you today? You won't even tell me why you broke up.'

She stayed silent so I dug deeper. 'I know something's not right. It's not been that way since your breakup. We were doing so well…'

'Ha! This you notice, but the last few years, when you should have…' she trailed off and I thought she was stopping, but she was only changing gears. 'What wasn't right…with you then?' Her interruption was scathing but it was on point.

My hands were hurting from clenching the wheel. It was the wrong time to bring it up but I was already too far down the rabbit hole. Besides, we had pulled into the driveway and I had nothing left in me but for the Hail Mary. 'Darlin', I know you're hurting—why wouldn't you go for counselling with me? It could help both of us.'

She was already halfway out of the car. 'Fat lot of good it did for you, Cynthia! All that schooling and you still didn't know what he was doing to me.'

'Babe…' I began. But she had already banged the car door and was storming into the house.

…I'm trying my best and all I want is for us to be friends, was what I had wanted to say.

I sat there motionless. Wave after wave of intense emotions swept over me. I was in a tortuous valley I wasn't able to navigate. *Every turn is either torturous or a cul-de-sac.*

◆

A few days later, Lily simply announced that she was going for her European sojourn with Joanna—it hadn't been posed as an idea or a question even. They had discussed it on their prom night—they were planning on backpacking across Spain for a couple of weeks and then Joanna would return. Lily was going to stay back in Barcelona to soak in the architecture and designs of Gaudí. She has inherited my love for architecture and I was glad our common love for the subject bound us in some way even in trying times. She has also inherited Connor's penchant for technology and is interested in pursuing a career at the intersection of both disciplines.

I had agreed with her decision to take a year off before college. I was still ambivalent about whether I had relented because of the guilt I felt for what she had gone through with Connor or because I actually thought it was a good idea. It's more likely to have been the former but I had rationalized that it would be good for her growth and happiness.

I was still torn though—happy she was going to embark on an experience of a lifetime but sad that none of it was going to be with me. I had considered floating the idea of travelling together again but hadn't been able to gather the gumption after the shutout of the last attempt. My contrition after the debilitating epiphany in Mr Dean's office hadn't done wonders for my courage either. At least her announcement had put me out of one of my miseries—that of wanting to bring up the topic again. I had been making consistent efforts to reconnect with Lily, but things between us hadn't improved one bit. I was at my wit's end.

◆

All Smiles

I could talk to James for hours. I had been able to do that ever since he had become my supervisor in school. Now that he has been my mentor through all my years of professional practice and we don't have to talk about assignments, exams and grades, our relationship has become more fulfilling. Our rendezvous are always too short for my liking, but the saving grace is I try to see him as often as possible. He constantly tells me I fuss over him way too much and I tell him it's not enough—he's good at taking care of everyone but himself.

It was nice and warm out, so I decided to take the scenic route to his place—through Times Square. While most New Yorkers abhor the gazillion tourists thronging the crossroads of the world and avoid it like the plague, I love stumbling right through the obstacle course. The novelty of the place has yet to wear off—I guess an advantage of neither being a native New Yorker nor living in the city.

I reminisced about my time in school, when James and I used to walk all the way from the NYU campus, through Times Square, to his place by the Park. While I would talk to him about the architecture and the history of the city, he would always bring me up to speed on trivia from the latest sci-fi movies. He is one of the few native New Yorkers who love everything about the city. His only peeve with Times Square is that it is now smoke-free.

It had been a while since I had seen him last. I could barely contain my excitement as I rang the doorbell.

◆

He greeted me like always—with a bear hug. I felt like I was in my dad's arms. He was wearing a light, white poncho and beige khakis. The attire complemented his glistening, gossamer hair—he always dresses elegantly.

'How are you doing, my darling?' He trumpeted in the all-too-familiar New York twang I've grown to love mostly because of him.

'Now I'm doing good!' I could feel the corners of my mouth reach for my ears.

He hobbled away, beckoning me to follow. I stopped smiling. 'What is this? Why are you limping?'

He muttered over his shoulder. 'Ah! It's just a trifle called old age, sweetie. Wouldn't worry about it.'

I was concerned. 'But it looks serious—have you been for a checkup recently?'

He turned around and looked at me sombrely. 'Yes! You're right. The doctors do recommend a very serious treatment, but I won't have it.'

'What is it?' I stopped dead in my tracks.

'A cane!' He let out a laugh like a twenty-two-year old instead of the sixty-seven he had on him.

'A cane?' I echoed incredulously, but he had already spun around.

'Now—come, come,' he hollered.

I followed him into his study and put his mail on his desk where he liked it, along with the medicines he had asked me to get.

'Oh, thank you so much—you are such a godsend.'

His study was less a study and more a perch with a glass curtain-wall overlooking the beautiful expanse of Central Park. It was his favourite spot at home, especially when he smokes his pipe. He maintains, 'If they don't let me smoke in the park, I'll smoke on top of it,' and always follows that with a guffaw. Thanks to the countless hours we have spent sitting around his drum-table, chatting while staring at the foliage, it has become my favourite spot too.

He poured us hot tea and pushed a tray of my favourite cookies towards me. His hand trembled as he raised the cup to his lips. 'So tell me, how've you been? How's Lily doing? Tell me how she's blossoming into a fine, young lady, now, won't you?'

In contrast with the levity of my thoughts, I tightened up. Lily was on top of my mind and I really needed his help. I recounted the incident at Principal Dean's office in detail. I also told him how, for the first time, seeing the shock on Principal Dean's face had made me realize my negligence. I couldn't believe she had been displaying these traits at home, in front of Connor, for more than two years and I had been oblivious to them. I tried, in fits and starts, to confess the guilt and shame I felt at having failed to protect my daughter from her own father. Previously, my guilt was from having discovered the abuse she had been subjected to. But after that day at school, my penitence had intensified. I should have seen the signs and prevented the abuse much sooner. I wondered why Lily had felt she couldn't talk to me or confide in me. In spite of my professional training, I had not the foggiest idea of how to get her to open up to me—I was at a complete loss.

This was personal—way too personal perhaps.

James gave me much more time to calm down than I usually afford my patients. And then, after the miasma had lifted, he dropped his shoulders, craned his neck, and looked me straight in the eyes. 'What good has this guilt done for you?'

Oh my god! When will I be able to mimic such sass so effectively in my sessions?

'Ha…ha!' is all that escaped me. I was at a loss as to what to say next, but he knew that.

'Your daughter went through a lot, but so did you. He treated you badly too, and when he realized he couldn't do that to you any more, he turned to a weaker prey. And your daughter was, and still is, just a girl. No one, not even you, could have imagined what a monster he-who-cannot-be-named is.'

Come to think of it, James does resemble Dumbledore. I liked that he couldn't bring himself to even say Connor's name.

'But there were all the telltale signs…' I began to protest.

He closed his eyes, raised his hand, and swayed back and forth slightly. 'Of course there were! But just like she couldn't say things for her own reasons, you couldn't see them for yours. Don't you get it—you both were in the same place and now you just need to find the same language.'

I remained quiet.

He answered my implicit question. 'My darling, all you have to do is talk to her. Tell her your side of the story. What better way to win her trust?'

I said, 'I've been trying so hard to be friends with her first.'

'Yeah, but friendship is based on something common—you have such a deep connection—use it.'

My inner critic was not satisfied. 'But how can I possibly justify not being able to see it? After all, it had been going on for almost three years. And it's not like I didn't know who he was—I must have just buried it somewhere deep inside.'

He lit the tobacco in his pipe. 'Hmm! Let me ask you this. Does Lily know how to ride a bicycle?'

I really didn't know where he was going with that. 'Yes.' In my head, however, it was meant to sound like a question.

'When did she learn how to ride?' he asked, before taking a puff from his pipe.

I tried to jog my memory. 'When she was fairly young... I think we removed her training wheels...'

'Do you remember her struggle? Her joy when she did her first hundred yards without the trainers?' he cut me off. I didn't mind. Our relationship was beyond that. When I would protest his interruptions at times, he would always quip he didn't know how much time he had left and he had to get it out of his system before it was too late. That, I did mind. And it had successfully stopped me from protesting.

I didn't think his rhetoric required a response.

'Do you remember her first fall, when she hurt herself?'

'Yeah...kind of,' I was still unsure of the point he was trying to make.

'What did she do then?'

I fought hard to remember. 'Well...she refused to get on the bike—no amount of cajoling and bribing got her back on; she just avoided it. For weeks, she would just walk past it not even acknowledging that it was…'

Whoa! Now that was a powerful metaphor. And simple! I wonder if he has a list of them somewhere?

I was on the edge of my seat, running the risk of toppling over onto the tea. My head was pounding and I could feel my pulse racing.

He delivered the coup de grâce. 'You see, when we get hurt by something, we avoid it till a catalysing event pushes us over and beyond the fear. As adults, our brains' autopilot finds it easier to feed the fear till it becomes insurmountable. So, we've got to make the brain get off its lazy butt and cross that event horizon!' he ended with a wink and a mischievous smile.

I smiled back. I knew that *Event Horizon* was one of his favourite sci-fi movies from the '90s, and he loved weaving movie names into regular conversations. *What a nerd!* I chastized myself, for having thought 'nerd' instead of 'geek'. 'A world of difference between the two,' he would have said. *How I wish I had half his elegance in addressing the most complex issues…*

My autopilot was still resisting. 'Yeah, but soon she's leaving for Spain for a few months.'

'What? No college?' he was clearly faking incredulity. 'Ah… teens! I'm so envious.' He knows exactly how to push my buttons and I thrive on it.

'Well, she has this hereditary obsession with Gaudí! She's going to imbibe his work, write a paper on some fancy applications of technology to his architectural style, and prepare her applications to college based on that experience. She's got it all figured out. I'm actually very proud of her.'

'As you should be. It's you she takes after,' he smiled.

I fell back into the chair so that he wouldn't catch me blushing.

'Ah! Forgive my interruption,' he continued. 'You were saying you would talk to her after…'

'Yeah, she's likely to forget.'

'Hmm!' He began stroking his Gandalf-like beard and looked at me obliquely.

I knew what he was going to say next.

'Or…' he said as if it were a question on my viva voce.

I don't mind being patronized by him. I offered what I hoped was a passing response. 'Or…continue to think about it while having a good time in Spain and, therefore, juxtapose our relationship with other positive mental stimuli.'

He laughed the same carefree laughter again. 'Now you know why you are my favourite.'

I knew he meant it. I thought of bringing up Lily's breakup with Roy but that was another thing I was clueless about. *First things first,* I told myself.

◆

On my way out, he asked, 'What about your practice—you've started again, right? How's it going?'

Ah! It hadn't even occurred to me to talk to him about my practice. 'Oh right! Things are going smoothly—it's good to be practising again. I have some regular patients who are progressing well…and some…irregular ones.'

We both laughed at our private joke—it was still fresh in spite of years of overuse. He was generous with his laughter as usual.

'There is one—of bereavement—my first after a long time.

It's quite sad actually—he lost his family in an accident and is really struggling with anger,' I said.

'That's quite natural. How long back was the accident?'

'That's the thing,' I said. 'It's going on more than seven months now, but he just started therapy. He's only been in for a couple of sessions so far.'

'Hmm… You've got to give it time…and so does he. What is he angry about?'

'It was a freak incident with no one else involved and he's looking to blame something or someone but can't pin it on anyone. He's not getting many answers from the police either, which hasn't helped.'

'Ah!' he said, adding, 'It's true what they say—you can begin to mourn only when you have your answers.'

'That's insightful! I'm definitely going to use it.' I knew I didn't need his permission. 'I also think he doesn't have many people to talk to, besides me. Our work is just beginning…'

'I'm sure you'll figure it out. Does he remember them fondly?'

'Who? The family? Well, he misses them.'

'Get him to remember them fondly—it breaks the anger pattern surprisingly well. It's also the litmus test for whether it's bereavement or mental illness.'

'That's a great idea! I will try and do exactly that,' I gave him a hug and a peck on his cheek and wished him goodbye. I turned around as I walked away—he was still looking at me. I hollered, 'Remember what Obama says—"Yes! You cane".' I knew he would relish the wordplay—he let loose that sumptuous laughter of his.

That's exactly how I wish to remember him, always.

'Come back soon. I don't think I see you enough,' he

shouted behind me. *Seeing him every day wouldn't be enough.*

My thoughts shifted to Sam. I made a mental note to get him to talk about his family and see how he handled that.

I was all smiles. I wondered how James does it but he always does!

◆

Memories

Sam's progress had been slow. He was still inconsistent with our sessions, often citing work as his reason to cancel. I hoped that work wasn't an excuse, because his behaviour was commensurate with his suffering. People can become inertial after the loss of a loved one. It was apparent he was just going through the motions of grieving, but I was still concerned about his inability to move beyond anger. Nonetheless, I was glad he was continuing our work together—he needed an environment where he felt understood and safe in order to break out of the anger pattern.

I was also glad he had resumed work, but as far as I could tell he was playing truant. He would schedule sessions just after lunch and would often come in smelling of beer. I wanted to cut him some slack but knew I had to watch out for any signs of substance abuse.

I was convinced that getting Sam to remember his family fondly would help him overcome his anger but hadn't been able to navigate us there. When he finally kept his next appointment, I attempted to force the subject again.

'Do you find yourself thinking about Marisa and William often?' I asked.

He looked up through slivers for eyes. 'Yeah! Of course—all the time.'

I felt reprimanded for the banality of my question but it was the best I could come up with.

'I wake up feeling afraid every morning,' he whispered after a few seconds.

Our patients assess us based on, amongst many things, the appropriateness of our metaphors and explanations. I offered, 'That's natural—the fear arises from the frustration of years of impulses, feelings, and actions that had your family as their object.'

I gave him a few seconds before asking, 'Do you feel like talking about them today?'

He bit on his lip before replying, 'Nah! It's too painful.'

It was the same response as that to my previous attempts at broaching the subject. I needed to break through that barrier and decided to employ a slightly aggressive tactic. It's somewhere on the cusp of sensitive questioning and constructive confrontation. I could gauge a patient's response and modulate my approach as we progress deeper into therapy. 'I think it might do you good. Besides, I don't know much about them.'

His grip around the armrest tightened and he continued looking at me through slit-eyes. 'And perhaps that's the way I'd like it to remain, Cynthia. Why don't you let me be the judge of what's good for me?'

It was…a tactic…not necessarily the best one.

I decided to relinquish control, a trifle. I also wanted to learn more about him. 'Why don't you tell me a little about yourself then? I mean your background—whatever you think is important to you.'

54

His grip loosened and his knuckles turned to red as he grappled with the context switch. He began after some time. 'I think I already told you I'm an only child, right?' He didn't wait for a response. 'I didn't grow up here—I've been here for the past twenty years or so and that too mostly because of Marisa, and then, Will.'

I still wasn't sure of his origin. In that moment, however, it was more important to let him drive the conversation and for me to navigate it to a happy place. I didn't interrupt him.

He seemed more comfortable with the new line of questioning. 'Growing up, I had all the love in the world and felt my parents provided more than I could have asked for.'

'It sure sounds like you had a great relationship with your parents,' I said. *It's always a positive sign—for the patient.*

'And I still do,' he replied. 'It's different with both of them—but still awesome—we always have fun together. I always imagined myself living close to them. They are still my first family…and now the only one…' he trailed off.

No! No! Think happy, Sam. I needed him to continue being positive for my new strategy to have a chance. 'You said you have fun together. Was it always that way—even while growing up?'

'Oh, absolutely! Some of my favourite memories are from my childhood—playing with them, going on trips, just chatting like I would with my friends.' He sounded cheerful for the first time.

'And would you do these kinds of things with Will as well?' I deliberately left his wife out, in order for the shift to be subtle.

He started squirming—a sign I had begun to read as being mostly favourable. I forced the subject directly. 'What are the kinds of things you would do with him?'

He stopped squirming, which had proven to be less favourable. *No? Not in that direction…*

55

I pushed differently. 'But…if you don't want to talk about it, then perhaps the kinds of things he liked?' I crossed my fingers under my notebook and ran my fingertips over the tiny tiles of its colourful embossment—it's my version of squeezing on a stress ball discreetly.

He perked up in the couch. 'Ah, Will! He was my sunshine. He liked everything. He could stay locked up in his room, building exciting new creations with his LEGO bricks. He loved being outdoors playing and…and helping me in the yard. He loved cycling with me and…oh yeah…going on road trips! Marisa was much more picky. He was crazy about science fiction—*Star Wars*, spaceships—you know the kind?' He looked at me obliquely.

That sounded like a question—one with subtext I didn't like. 'Mm…hmm! I'm not that old Sam,' I said with a smile.

'Ha! Ha! No, that's not what I meant,' he said, his face turning red. 'He was a nerdy kid!'

'I believe the word you're looking for is geeky!' The words escaped my mouth before I knew it.

He froze. Then laughed.

Phew! I uncrossed my fingers under my notebook.

For the first time, he had stopped snapping and was smiling unreservedly. 'That's what he used to say. Six of one, half a dozen of the other buddy, is how I would riposte. Ha! Ha! I guess you're right.'

'About the geeky bit—yes I am!' I was confident because I had it on good authority.

'No! About not being that old,' he said winking.

I was glad he was my patient or else he would have found himself on the wrong side of my right fist. I laughed. Not doing so would have meant acknowledging a fact I spend significant time avoiding—that I'm now on the wrong side of forty. 'You're messing with fire, Sam, messing with fire,' and then I waited for a few seconds, before winking back.

He was laughing by then. 'I don't know how many trips we had made together to the Intrepid here by Pier Eighty-Six.'

I had gone there once with James, had enjoyed it, and had wanted to take Lily too. But I hadn't been able to convince her yet.

Sam was finally opening up. 'His favourite was our trip to the Kennedy Space Centre. We had gone to Disney World with a couple of family friends and their kids. They had all left after the weekend and we had stayed back in Orlando for a road trip to the Space Centre.'

'Marisa hadn't been too happy but we had worked our charm...or let's say emotional blackmail...on her. He had absolutely loved it. In fact, she had enjoyed it as well. Our plan had been to spend a few hours there but we ended up going in for the whole shebang. There was just so much to see...and do!'

I felt a mini wave of relief—it's one I feel each time my patients make the tiniest of breakthroughs—it's almost always tiny and builds up slowly.

His own wave was that of excitement and it continued cresting. 'It was our first IMAX together. It was pretty impressive. He had loved being out there to see the launch pad and the buildings where the rockets are built. It's almost impossible to imagine the size of those buildings till you've seen them with your own eyes.' He had leaned back and raised his arms wide above his head. 'What he had enjoyed most was the shuttle launch experience. It's very realistic. Have you been? If you get a chance, you must—totally worth every penny!'

It was the first time I was seeing this boyish, excitable side of Sam. I wasn't about to bridle it.

Then he seemed to stiffen. 'We must have been the last ones to leave, because there weren't any cars in the parking lot when we finally got done. And then... Ha! Ha!' His smile was a little crooked; almost sinister. *Must be my imagination.*

'Then our car wouldn't start. Man, was she pissed! With her, I was always landing from the frying pan into the fire. We had to wait for triple-A to show up and to contend with Mrs Hufflepuff—Ha! Ha!—our code name for her. I think she knew about it though. Thankfully, I had Will to distract me. He just wouldn't shut up about all the cool things he had learned and had so many questions. I didn't know the answers to most of them and really had to improvise. We all had the ice cream that the astronauts have up there in space.' He pointed his finger upwards. 'I had to go with Marisa on this one—it was pretty bad. He didn't care—he polished off all three of them.'

Then his enthusiasm ebbed again. But I was happy—it was an important milestone after all.

He slowed down for the first time in a few minutes. 'There was so much that needed to be done...and said. You know... I find myself wishing it was me and not him...not them...'

It was a delicate moment. I needed to avoid any platitudes, but still wanted to turn his attention to the future. I kept my hand on his. 'After a loss like yours, you have to start everything again—learn how to walk, dream, and even trust again—while remembering the past as beautifully as you can. It's never easy.'

He nodded.

I was happy he was finally able to reminisce and talk about them fondly. *Is this the breakthrough he needed?*

◆

58

Breakdown

That afternoon I had one more session, which was also intense. I was, however, looking forward to a date later in the evening. It wasn't my first since Connor and I had separated, but I hadn't been on many. Not memorable ones anyway. My friends had tried convincing me it was about time I started putting myself out there, but I hadn't paid much heed. It was only when James said I needed to look after myself, even in order to affect positive outcomes on my relationship with Lily, that I began to see light in the argument.

I had been informed by reliable sources that people didn't meet at bars any longer. In fact, I had been laughed at for asking if they still met at church. Of course, I had been joking! Online dating apps are apparently the way to go. I had quickly discovered I was all thumbs, not only when it came to technology but also when it came to picking dates through the use of such technology. Lost between swiping in all directions, I didn't even remember the name of my date that night. But my nerves still felt like jello—like they're supposed to before a first date—and I kinda liked it.

◆

I was lost in never-never land as I was leaving my office building. I barely noticed him. He was sitting in a ball, huddled up on his haunches, right outside on the street. Something about his wrist sticking out struck me as oddly familiar.

It was Sam's wrist. I could tell from the frayed friendship bands. 'Sam!' I exclaimed in disbelief.

What is he doing here?

He looked up through bloodshot eyes. He had clearly just collapsed there and had been crying for the past hour. For all its charm, that's the one thing I don't get about this city—*how could a man have just sat there crying in plain sight and have not one person care enough to have checked up on him! To be fair, it isn't just this city now, is it?* I crouched right next to him, put one arm around his shoulders and offered to lift him up with the other. 'C'mon, get up. Let's go inside.'

From the corner of my eye, I stole a quick glance at my watch. I had a few minutes before I needed to catch the next train back and make it for my date in time.

I brought him back into the lobby, told him not to move, and went to bring him a soda—it helps in taking some of the edge off. As he began to calm down, he found his voice. 'I'm sorry... I really couldn't take it any more... I just miss him so goddamn much.' His head was hung low and he was squelching his eyes with his palms.

'Of course you do. They meant everything to you. I know it's painful and you needn't be sorry—to anyone.' I needed him to come to terms with a way of expressing grief other than anger. 'It's okay to be who you want to be, to feel what you naturally do, even to be a bit crazy...in a safe environment.'

He looked up at me. 'Crazy! What do you mean by crazy?'

I was afraid he might have misunderstood me. 'No! By crazy,

I don't mean deranged... I mean...everyone's way of handling grief is different, and you need a lot of space and understanding from your environment.'

'But you said safe too... What does that mean?'

Neither was I expecting such a stark change in demeanour nor a barrage of questions. 'I mean...as long as you don't hurt yourself or others.'

He tugged at his beard. 'Hmm...hurt...that's broad... we're all hurting...in some way or the other... Never mind!'

'Where are you going with this, Sam?' I asked, growing slightly concerned.

'Well...you said crazy...and I wasn't sure what you meant... And where you'd draw the line? You also said I needn't be sorry.'

I wished I hadn't asked where he was going with that. He had been willing to let it go.

He came to my rescue. 'But really! Never mind. I'll figure it out sooner or later.' He waved the subject off.

That time, I was happy to let him. Not because I didn't have any answers but more so because I was getting really late. An hour or so ago, I was happy for his breakthrough. At that moment, I wasn't certain. 'I'm concerned about you...'

'No, no! Don't be. I'll be okay,' he interrupted. 'I'm sorry... I mean I'm not!' He laughed a little and the soda sputtered out. 'I mean you should go. I'll be okay. Really.'

'Were you on your way home?' I asked.

'I was but I didn't get too far, now, did I?' he laughed some more.

I was a little perturbed by his erratic behaviour, but I was relieved to see him smile again. As I watched him walk away, I made a mental note to check in on him later.

◆

Even though I made it to my date on time, I can't say it was the most inspired evening or choice of restaurant for that matter. While it's possible that Sam's capricious catharsis continued to trouble me, it's more likely that I was consumed by how much I was going to miss Lily who was leaving soon. To be honest though, I didn't know where I'd much rather be—subjecting myself to Lily's ire or dining at that seedy restaurant.

Meh! At least I had dressed up and felt good about myself—a feeling long overdue.

◆

Dredging the Past

Although I felt emboldened after meeting James, I hadn't been able to bring up my past with Lily. I had scripted what I was going to say and played the conversation in my mind a hundred times but my bravado got sandwiched between her aggression and my apprehensions. I kept letting opportunities slip until there were only a few days before she left for her vacation. That she had joined a girls-only, architecture-and-technology interest group, had immersed herself in researching colleges, and was spending all her free time with Joanna wasn't helping my cause either.

One day, while she was helping me with the groceries, I took a leap of faith. 'Hon! I need to speak with you about something.' When I didn't get a response, I looked over my shoulder. Her back was towards me and her head was bobbing to the punk noise she referred to as music. I wondered if she would ever get over that phase. *Now that she is spending so much time with Joanna, perhaps there's hope,* I told myself.

As soon as she turned around, I waved to get her attention. She took one of the earphones out, raised her brows, and said, 'Yes?'

'I need to speak with you,' I said.

'Sure! What about?'

'It's about Connor.'

She put the colourful box of Froot Loops on the counter and finally switched off the music. 'Not sure if I can,' she said. 'I've barely been able to get him out of my mind and you want to talk about him. As far as I'm concerned, there's nothing to talk about.'

I squeezed the peach in my hand to keep myself from hyperventilating. 'But there is. There's so much you need to know.'

'No! There's nothing more for me to know. I was there, remember?'

My head was already hurting. I didn't want to talk about it either but I hadn't been able to come up with any other way of correcting the course of our life together. 'I know dear…and I know he hurt you…but I was there too and I desperately need to get some things off my chest. I need you to talk to me. I want to understand…'

She grabbed the box of cereal and spun around to put it away in the cabinet. 'What's there to understand, Mother? He hit me…and then he hit me some more…and then he continued hitting me for a very long time. That would have been a good time to talk. What's the point of talking about it now?'

I had to persist, calmly. 'The point is that I want you to know why I didn't see it sooner, love. I want to know why you…'

She slammed the cabinet door. 'Why I what, Mother? It was your job to protect me. Now I know he is an angry, drunk loser, but what about you? You're supposed to know how the human mind works or something like that, right? Where were you? Why weren't you doing your job?'

The tension between us was palpable, and the peach in my hand was bearing the brunt of it. 'That's exactly what I want to explain to you.'

She screeched. 'Explain! There's no point of any explanations now. What was required then was action, and you failed. How's that for an explanation?' She stormed away towards the stairs leading up to her bedroom, but stopped short. Without looking back, she said, 'Maybe some day we'll be ready to talk about this, but not now.'

Her faith gave me strength for one last push. 'Okay!' I succumbed. 'Can you please not walk away at least? Can we talk about something else then?'

'Like what?' she asked, without looking back.

I hadn't thought it through so I improvised. 'Perhaps we can talk about college—would love to know what you've found out so far.'

She looked up towards her bedroom, sighed, and then relented. 'All right. What do you want to know?' She swivelled and walked back towards me.

I waited for her to get back to the island. 'I know you've been researching colleges—what are you thinking?'

Without looking at me, she said, 'I'm not sure yet—I'm looking at options both on the West Coast and out here as well.'

I had to stop my heart from beating out of its cavity. I couldn't bear the thought of her moving away—not just then. It could be my last shot at building something meaningful with her.

She continued, 'My top choice on the West Coast is UCLA and out here it's NYU, but I'm also interested in one in Boston.'

I could sense she wanted to get away and I knew pushing her in any direction meant only one thing—pushing her away from me. I took solace in the fact that NYU, my alma mater, was

65

at least a contender. It was a situation that warranted handling with kid gloves and I found myself wishing I hadn't broached that topic either. 'So, how do you plan to decide?'

'Hmm…am not sure…still doing my research and will decide while I'm in Spain. I plan to send out some applications while I'm there.'

I was already out on a limb and I reached a little further. 'Do you feel like discussing it now? I could help.'

She started squirming. 'Umm…not really.' She looked over my head at the clock. 'Oh! Would you look at the time? I'm sorry but I promised Joanna I would pick her up and I'm already running late now. Sorry! Gotta run… see you later.'

And then, she scooted out the door. And with her, so did my shot at a confession and possible end to my torment. I had little choice but to reconcile with the idea of sharing my past with her after her return. *James would not have approved.*

◆

Send-off

Before I knew it, the day I had been dreading was upon me—Lily was leaving for almost ten weeks. In the days leading up to her departure, I had focused all my energy on trying to stay as upbeat as possible. I knew she needed anything but a moping mother. On that day, however, a few hours before I was to take Joanna and her to the airport, I wasn't doing my best. I felt an agonizing numbness. We were having lunch in silence and I had been toying with the pasta when she finally broke the tension by muttering.

I was startled out of my daze. 'Huh?'

'I said, are you okay? You're just playing with your food.'

'Mm…hmm… I'm excited for you…it's just…' I thought the rest of it in my head…*that…I'm plummeting down a precipice and don't know how to ask for help.*

'I know, right? *Estoy muy feliz también,*' she said she was happy too.

Yeah I know. I think her confident Spanish diction was what broke my fall and I let out a feeble laugh.

She talked about her plans and how happy she was that

Joanna had decided to join her for a couple of weeks. Then she went upstairs to finish packing.

This is what I wanted right…to talk about plans around the island… But I was still very sad. Damn the island!

◆

I had insisted on dropping her to the airport. I wanted to stick to her like a leech. After finishing my lunch, I went to her bedroom and sat on her bed watching her pack. It didn't take me more than a few seconds to realize that the jarring sounds blaring from her stereo were drowning my emotions! I couldn't feel pain. Come to think of it, I couldn't feel anything and I was thankful for it! I did manage to construct at least one coherent thought—*she is brave—I don't think I could have done what she is doing.*

When she was done, I took the larger suitcase and she brought up the rear with the carry-on. As we rolled them towards the stairs in silent unison, the mollycoddling mother kicked in. 'Have a safe flight, my love, and let me know as soon as you land and also when you have a number there.' Without pausing for breath, I continued, 'You must message me every day to let me know you're okay.'

'Yes, Mother!' Ironically, that's the only time she called me that—when she wanted me to stop mothering. In fact, I could picture her rolling her eyes and shaking her head. I wish I hadn't turned around to check, because that's when it happened.

The suitcase was still pulling me forward. When I turned around to look at her, I tripped and fell. The suitcase stole away from me and dove down the stairs. I dove after it, landing atop it. *Now, I was really falling down a precipice.* Then, I overtook it. And the tumbling began. All the while, I could hear Lily screaming. *Why is she screaming? I'm the one falling.*

'Thud!' The suitcase landed on my ankle and I yelped in pain.

Oh! That's why the screaming. She was trying to warn me. *Is it broken? I'm sure it is.*

She came scampering down. 'Oh my! Are you okay, Mom?'

The irony continues—now she calls me Mom. It felt like receiving a trophy…for coming in last.

She heaved the suitcase aside. 'Don't move! Wait! Let me see.'

Her hands felt good on my ankle, but other memories were already haunting me. It wasn't the first time I had fallen down those very stairs. *Of course, the last time I hadn't fallen as much as I had been…* I couldn't even bring myself to think it.

My Lily had donned her Florence Nightingale cape and was in full control. She dragged the beanbag from the living room and propped me against it. She brought ice in a Ziploc and it was slumped around my throbbing ankle. She even got an elastic bandage from upstairs. All of this with her cell phone tucked between her ear and her shoulder as she instructed Joanna to come pick her up instead.

'Does it hurt when I move it?' she asked, gently moving my ankle.

In a bid to put up a brave front, I said, 'Only slightly.'

'It's not broken.' She proceeded to start wrapping it up.

That's my daughter! I thought proudly. I would have been able to control myself had it not been for how gentle she was with me. Her soothing touch and voice broke through my defences and I was bawling like a baby.

'What? Is it hurting?' she asked, stopping the bandaging.

I shook my head. My whole body was shivering because of all the emotions coursing through it.

69

'What then, Mom? I don't think it's broken. Will you be okay?'

'Mm…hmm…' was all I could get out.

'You sure this is not a trick to keep me back, right?' she said with a smile.

We both laughed.

'Yes, yes! I think I will be okay. See, I can move it already,' I said wincing, but she was looking at my foot.

'I'm so sorry, darlin',' I blurted.

'Sorry for what, Mom? You didn't do anything.' I was already getting accustomed to her calling me that, but I didn't think getting injured was a sustainable strategy to ensure it.

Then…it all came tumbling out… 'He hit me too, you know.'

'Who did?' she asked.

'Connor…who else?' The moment it was out of my mouth, I stopped shivering.

She fell back on the bottom step.

I couldn't stop myself and it all came out steadily, albeit in between whimpers. 'It was a long time back… You must have been ten or eleven perhaps.' I had buried it so deep, I couldn't be sure.

'I think it happened when you were at a sleepover.'

'We were upstairs. We had an argument about something and it got out of hand. One thing led to another and he flung the TV remote at me. I couldn't get out of the way and it hit me squarely in the chest. I was really afraid.'

'I backed away…asked him to calm down…and said I was going downstairs. But he followed me out of the bedroom…'

I was boiling. I could feel the ice melting around my ankle.

'…and at the top of the stairs, he held me by the arm

70

and pulled me back really viciously. I told him he was hurting me, but he just kept twisting my arm. I threatened to call the police...and he let go for a second.'

I was still sobbing profusely, but I knew I just had to get it all out.

'I started coming down the stairs and I remember saying something like... "You should control yourself".

'That's when I think he lost it again. He came bounding down the stairs, screaming, and pushed me... He pushed me down...'

By this time, my throat was parched, yet I felt wet and sweaty. I wondered if Lily remembered the time when my right arm had been in a cast for a month. I had covered up the incident with a lie.

'I knew he had been struggling with work, but what he did was just wrong. I thought of calling the police or my parents but I kept making excuses. Then I guess... I guess it just got buried somewhere...'

I finally looked up at her. She had her elbows on her knees, with the fingers of both her hands fanned out across her cheeks. Her mouth was open and she was just staring back at me.

'But I did muster enough courage, one day soon after, to tell him what he had done was absolutely unacceptable and I wouldn't stand for it. If he ever laid a finger on me again, I would go straight to the police.'

'Now that I think of it...I should have gone then... It would have saved both of us so much trouble.'

I had barely finished the sentence, when I heard the sharp sound of a horn from outside. Joanna was there to pick her up. I felt Lily stirring. I needed to say so much more to her but all I could get out was, 'I could never have imagined Lily... He

71

was always angry and mean…but I had learned to live with it. It didn't matter much after you were born anyway. I had you—I had everything I could have ever wanted in my life.'

She looked like a deer caught in headlights. More like a caribou really, because of her spikes.

'Why didn't you say something before?' she said, but any chance of a longer, more meaningful mother-daughter moment was thwarted by the piercing sound of the horn, only more persistent then.

'Mom! This is too much…just way too much for me right now. I can't handle it—not at this time.'

She buzzed around like a bee and dragged her suitcases out. Then, from the doorway, looking straight back at me, she said, 'I wish you would have told me all this before… I don't know what to do with this now.'

And then…just like that…she was gone.

I sat there crying—tears rolling down my cheeks and, it felt, all the way down to my ankle.

I was still in a stupor when my cell phone beeped. She had left it right next to me before leaving.

It was a message from her. 'I'm sorry I had to rush out. Please take care of yourself. Will miss you.'

No Mom. No Cynthia.

I'll take what I can get.

◆

Salvage

If I had been surprised to see him outside my office on the street the other day, then it's safe to say I was flabbergasted when I opened the door to let him into my office for his next session. In fact, I may have even let out a shriek. He was wearing the same clothes—his street clothes—and he was reeking! I didn't know which I found more disconcerting—his appearance or his smell.

'Good lord! What hole did you fall into?' he asked, as he followed me in.

I found his question not only ironic but also moronic—I should have been asking him that! I assumed it was his way of asking after my injured ankle. 'Oh! It's nothing really.'

'You don't say! It doesn't look like nothing to me. What happened?'

He was right—it wasn't nothing. It had turned out to be a hairline fracture and I was hobbling hopelessly. *Those stairs would be the death of me,* I thought. 'I tripped and fell while descending some steps, but it's just a hairline.'

'Just a hairline? Then why does that look like a bomb shelter?

You sure you okay?'

Ominous as it was, I hadn't heard my cast being referred to as that. I laughed at his hyperbole. 'Yeah! I will be, soon. Thanks for your concern.' He sounded sincere—it was endearing.

◆

As it turned out, he had a couple of surprises in store for me too. He delivered them in quick succession. 'I'm doing much better,' he said, following it up with, 'I've decided to pack up and leave.'

I did a double take at these unexpected proclamations; for one, he definitely didn't look any better and, for another, his decision didn't exactly sound like it was well thought through. I was at a loss, not knowing what to say, and quite possibly should have said more than just 'Okay.'

'Everything reminds me of Will and I just can't get him out of my mind,' he confessed.

As if by some miracle designed to give me a moment to gather my wits, his phone rang and he took it out of his pocket. I hoped he would pick it up to talk, buying me a little more time, but he promptly disconnected it and put it on the couch next to him. It was an iPhone—an older model—the design of its case was an asymmetric mosaic of blue tiles. It took me an instant to place it. It was a distinctive Gaudí mosaic pattern—one that I loved. I couldn't believe the coincidence. I wondered if he had noticed the dragon on my notebook—it had been staring right at him during all our sessions. *Perhaps he is oblivious to the treasure that is Gaudí*, I thought. In that moment, I may have judged him. That's when I noticed the cracked screen—a cruel metaphor for my foot and his soul. I wondered if the crack was from its fall in the plane and he hadn't gotten around to fixing it. *After all, why would he have, when he isn't even looking after himself?*

At least he wasn't angry any more. I wondered if he had moved to bargaining or was nosediving towards depression at a frenetic pace. If it was bargaining, I would have expected it to manifest as self-blame. Grieving is strange that way—you never know what it throws up.

It's not that I was concerned that his leaving was a bad decision, but rather that decisions such as these, especially when made in haste and whilst in dismay, seldom result in anything but regret.

He apologized for the interruption before continuing, 'Without him...everything and everyone...looks so shabby and worn out. I just can't deal with it—with the loneliness and the longing. After all, I had moved here for her and may have even moved back had it not been for Will. Now...I have nothing holding me back.'

What does he mean by 'moved back had it not been for Will'?

'I just want it to be over, Cynthia,' he sighed deeply as he said that.

Just the opening I need, I thought. 'The loss is clearly very hard for you, but grief is not a disease you can get over, Sam. The goal is not to forget but to reconcile. It's okay...if that's what you've decided but...'

He looked at me as if he was searching for salvation. I had to search too, albeit for the right summation. 'But is that what you need?'

I wasn't going to be the first one to break the silence.

'Hmm...' is all he offered at first. And then, 'Well, you did say I shouldn't be afraid of doing something crazy.' His brows jumped up and remained there.

I ignored his bait. 'You have a business here you clearly love.' I knew I was reaching. I still didn't know what he did for a living or where he was originally from. That's the irony of this profession—we get intimate with our patients, but it's in facets of their lives mostly of their choosing.

'Ah! But the business pretty much takes care of itself. It's technology and you know how it is with technology these days—everything can be done remotely.'

I didn't know how it was with technology and, besides, I did want him to talk through his decision. 'Where were you thinking of going—back home to your parents?'

He went back to hemming and hawing, so I continued, 'What do you have there to look forward to, besides family of course?'

'That's the thing—that's what I might be looking forward to the least,' he said with a slight laugh. 'I mean, don't get me wrong. I love my family but I'm not sure I can contend with hers too. After the funeral, when they were all here...phew! I don't know... I don't think I can...or even want to handle that. I have some really good friends there... Perhaps what I really need is a distraction...'

I had hoped that my question about his family would have allowed me to learn more about him, but his response truncated that possibility. Besides, his last comment was the segue I needed to help him consider alternatives other than just packing up and leaving. I volunteered, 'Have you considered a vacation... to some place...doing something fun like cycling? It could do you a world of good.'

He perked up. 'You know, that's not a bad idea at all.' Then he slouched back and looked away. 'But I'm not sure about taking a vacation alone.'

I wanted to encourage him. 'You could ask that friend of yours... John, was it?' I surprised myself by having remembered his name, but I still had only a few regular patients and the details weren't all muddled.

He shot a glance in my direction. 'Have I told you about him? Huh! I didn't know I had. Well... I'm not sure if I'm ready for that either... Let me think about it. That does remind me of something else I've been meaning to talk to you about, though.'

Given the pace at which he had been ambling away from anger, I didn't think avoidance was the best idea. I pushed a little harder. 'Sure, we can talk about whatever is on your mind, but why don't you think you are ready for a vacation with a friend?'

He stared at me for a moment. 'I said I'd think about it. Let me do that, please.'

I persisted pleasantly. 'Are you sure you're not just trying to change the topic?'

He continued staring for a second or so, but then his expression softened enough to allow for a smile. 'Perhaps... But what I have to tell you is important.'

I wasn't about to give in so easily, not without a negotiation at least. 'Okay! But can we agree you'll talk your decision through with me, before acting on it?'

He murmured something and then finally said, 'All right! I can do that. Now can I tell you about these strange dreams I keep having?'

◆

SALVAGE

Nightmares

I was ready to move on to talk about his dreams. I hoped he could move on as well, without having to move back. 'Sure, tell me about these dreams.'

'They're nightmares really, and I can't get them to stop.' He sighed deeply. 'They first started with gory scenes of the accident…of the site…which is weird because I still haven't seen it. I would always wake up sweating…and couldn't go back to sleep. Then, after a while, the dreams changed. I could see both of them hovering over me and trying to speak to me, to reach out to me, and touch me with their hands… But they couldn't… as if there was some kind of invisible shield stopping them.'

He paused. Thinking that was the end of it, I was about to suggest keeping a dream journal. It had helped quite a few of my patients.

But he continued, 'For the past few days these visions have disappeared. Now it's a different theme, but it's a recurring one and just as haunting. I still wake up…in desperation. In my dream as well, I'm woken up by a really loud ring… It's a phone…it's my phone!' He grimaced and raised his hands to his ears, as if he was trying to block the insistent ringing out that very second.

'I'm still groggy but I grab it to make the ringing stop.' He reached to pick up an imaginary phone. 'All I hear is heavy breathing…and then finally, when someone speaks…I can't tell whose voice it is. And I mean, not in the way that I can't recognize whose voice it is, but I can't even tell if it's a person or…something else.'

He was breathing heavily—as if he was living his nightmare right then. 'It has a strange feminine quality to it…but…but it's also almost metallic. I ask who it is but I get nothing. Then after a while…when it speaks again…all it says is, "I know why… I know how…", and click! It hangs up. That's when I wake up…gasping…as if someone had been trying to strangle me.'

He waited for his panting to subside. 'It's always so stressful…and as much as it pains me to be in the dream, all I want to do is go back right into it… I don't even know why. I didn't make too much of it when I had it for the first time, but then it just refuses to go away.'

He had mentioned this need before as well, but it had been buried under anger, which had been an impediment to his healing. The accuracy of our interpretations matter immensely to our patients, but what matters more is how we push them outside their comfort zones. 'That does sound stressful—why do you think you want to go back into the dream?'

'I already said I don't know!' he shot back. 'I'm hoping you will tell me…'

'Could it be because you want to know what the voice has to say?'

He almost jumped. 'Oh yeah! I'd like to know…interrogate her…it…whatever…'

79

I knew it was time again to ask the question he had evaded in the past. 'Tell me—did you ever end up going back to the police? To find out if anything new had come up? Any new developments?'

I assumed he hadn't. 'Perhaps your subconscious is trying to suggest you need more answers—that you need to go find out how it happened. Maybe you've been afraid to find out and have been avoiding it, and that's exactly the purpose you need.'

I thought I saw the start of a smile, but he started speaking too quickly. 'I don't think any good can come from that... I need more than the police.'

I needed to challenge him to help him acknowledge his need. That is how we promote self-understanding—by encouraging patients to take some risks. When he didn't say anything else for almost a minute, I offered, 'How would you know till you try? Grief is not passive, Sam. It is what you do to heal yourself. You have to listen to what your subconscious is telling you, follow it, and then give it time.'

He began squirming. Again, I became aware of how much he was stinking.

James's words rang in my head—something about making the 'brain get off its lazy butt'—I decided to throw in challenge number two. 'I feel I have come to know you a little. You don't strike me as someone who backs down from a challenge. And sometimes, when we come up against a wall, we've got to plant our roots deep down like a tree and grow over the wall to get to a better place—a place from where we can see more clearly.'

He stopped fidgeting. His eyes were alight and wide. I took it as a sign of a deep epiphany and pushed harder. 'We often believe, and rightly so, that all answers are to be found within. But sometimes we need to put ourselves out there and go looking for them outside too.'

His expression changed. I felt I had broken through.

He looked into the distance and spoke for the first time since I had begun my monologue. 'I think you might be on to something... It's okay to be a bit crazy...and I don't need to be sorry...if it helps me grow...over the wall...to a better place...'

'Exactly!' I echoed.

He was smiling, unreservedly. 'Thank you!' he said.

I felt I could talk to him more as an ally rather than as an adviser. In fact, we even chatted a little, almost like friends—a first for our sessions. The session with Sam was my last one that day and I had let it run longer—enough to have to hurry if I were to catch the next train back home. I decided to leave the office with him. As I followed him out, I felt for the first time that he was actually moving forward—he was not just thinking about the past, but also looking at the future. And we had his nightmares to thank for it.

◆

Sparring

I wrestled with the lock while hopping on one leg. He chivalrously offered to hold my bag. 'How're you going to get home with that?'

'With what?' I asked. 'You mean the bomb shelter? It is going to be bit of a drag, but I think I'll survive!'

He laughed. 'You'll take the train?'

'Yeee…ah!' *Had I told him that?*

'No you won't,' he said with a straight face.

'What do you mean I won't? You should know better than to mess with a woman and her crutch.' I waved my weapon at him menacingly.

'Ha! Ha!' He had a boisterous laugh. 'I meant I'll drive you home.'

Given my state of indisposition, I was tempted to jump at the offer. But then the prospect of occupying quarters, smaller than even my office, with smelly Sam wafted into my mind and I wasn't so sure. 'No…I couldn't possibly impose.'

'Not an imposition at all.' He assured me that my place wasn't much of a detour and beckoned me to follow.

It was likely that I was going to miss the next train back anyway. So the choice was really between waiting forty-five minutes on the platform and driving for about the same time with him. At least this way I'd be home sooner. I relented. Besides, he was holding my handbag hostage on his shoulder.

I hopped in line behind him. Strangely, I felt a wave of sadness swell over me. I was sure it wasn't because of the session. Although we had started on a morose note, we had been able to swing things around rather well.

◆

As he held the door open for me to hop into his car, I noticed it was a gorgeous summer afternoon and that perked me up a bit. Oozing through the city traffic, I took in the festive crowd making its way into Bryant Park for the Monday night movie. They were showing *The Usual Suspects*, one of my all-time favourites. Soon, the Chrysler building—another favourite— came into view and I craned to get a full glimpse. My daily walk between the station and my office didn't take me all the way up to it. I could barely discern the silhouettes of the gargoyles protruding from the cornices but they reminded me how much I missed Lily. I realized the swell of sadness a few minutes earlier had been because I was missing her—she had been gone for a few weeks and we had only spoken on the phone a couple of times.

'That is one beautiful building,' he said, breaking the silence and, along with it, the waves of sadness.

'Oh! I couldn't agree more,' I said, still looking out.

He fired the first salvo. 'The things people do to get noticed, eh?'

'What do you mean?' I asked.

'That spire on top—do you know it was constructed secretly inside the building? The builders didn't want anyone to find out they were going after the record for the world's tallest building at the time. Apparently, it was installed in just about ninety minutes.'

Okay…I didn't know that, I thought, feeling bested. So…I lied. 'Ha! I know what you mean.' More a prevarication really!

'Of course you do! What was I thinking? I've seen all the books in your office. How's that again?'

'My dad was an architect,' I told him. 'He used to bring me to work with him often. He would always take a different route, we would walk hand-in-hand, and he would tell me fascinating stories behind New York's finest buildings on our way over. It was my first love…in a way.'

I wanted to go back to sparring—it was a matter of pride. 'It is still the world's tallest brick building.'

'On a steel frame, it is!' He wasn't backing down. And my ego was taking a pummelling.

'And you? How do you know all this trivia?' I had to find out.

'Ha! Ha! I guess you can say it comes with the job.'

I thought he was in technology. 'Say more.'

'My company—we develop all kinds of software—one of our products is a CAD…'

'I'm sorry, a what?' I interrupted him.

'Well, it's an architecture and design software. I end up working with a lot of architects and since I don't know much about architecture per se, knowing all these tidbits helps me connect better with them. First, they throw all these sophisticated terms at me and I just nod. Then, when it's my turn, I regale them with stories and trivia. It's not exactly a match made in heaven, but we make it work!'

'Ha! Ha! Smooth,' I meant it as a compliment, but I had lost my chutzpah to go head to head with him on that topic.

Other than my bruised ego, the outcome of the rest of the drive was pleasant. He managed to lift my spirit with his banter. I was grateful he had insisted on dropping me home. I may even have been a bit disappointed that the traffic had cooperated so well—we were outside my place in no time. Waving to him as he drove away, I became aware of another woe that had been idling for a while—the lack of intimacy.

◆

Whirling around on my driveway, that void was underscored by the sight of my empty nest. My original heartache from missing the love of my life, Lily, returned.

I had an email for her that had been sitting in my drafts. I wanted to review it one last time before sending it out.

Lily, my darling—about what I shared with you before you left—I'm sorry for having shared it then. You were right. It wasn't the best time to do that and it definitely wasn't part of a plan. I realized my mistake— that of being oblivious to your plight—only a little while back. I had been trying to share all of it with you but kept failing. The sadness because of you leaving and my fall—they just broke me I guess. And I thought it was just my ankle!

I pray we have all the time left in the world as mother and daughter, but more

85

importantly, as best friends. However, there are some things I must tell you now. After Connor hit me, I tried really hard to forget it—partly because of my own fears and partly because I hoped to preserve some semblance of family life for us. I know now, I was wrong in doing so. I guess I ended up spending so much time and energy escaping from my own reality that I was unable to see that he was doing it to you as well.

But there is no excuse—absolutely none—for having been blind to what you were being put through. For that, I'm ashamed and most importantly, sorry for having failed you, my love.

I wish I could go back in time and do things differently. I wish I could go back in time and punish him. But I can't. All I can do is learn, and hope, and work hard at giving us another chance to build a meaningful relationship—for as long as I'm alive.

Love,
Your friend forever,
Cynthia

I vacillated between signing off as Mom and Cynthia, but settled on the safer bet.

◆

Glass Everywhere

Over the next couple of months, Sam started overcoming his anger and showing steady signs of healing. I was happy for him but progress was still uneven. He was coming in for our sessions consistently and enjoying his work. He was even cycling and appeared to be losing weight. He was taking better care of himself and it showed.

It had taken some cajoling, but he had finally renewed his quest for some answers. 'I went back to the police,' he told me during one of our sessions. 'It was tough.'

'I'm sure it was.'

'I met the same officer…the sheriff…Matthews. He had just returned from a vacation, but was understanding and helpful. He asked me if I felt ready to go see the site. I wasn't, to be honest, but I found myself nodding. We drove in silence. It was really difficult to tell if there had ever been any accident… until we walked down to the…tree…where…' he was already choking up.

He continued after a pause, 'There was tall grass all around, but I could still see glass everywhere… Millions of shards…

almost like stars…only not. The tree was pretty banged up too…thank god, there was no…no sign of any blood… Don't think I could have handled that. I fell to my knees…he had to literally lift me up…' he said, hoisting an imaginary person with both his hands, '…before we could go back to the car.'

I held his outstretched palm and pressed it gently. He reciprocated before continuing. 'On the way back, Matthews told me that their suspicion of instant death had been confirmed. They had both been dislodged because of the fall…' he trailed off.

It was some time before he resumed. 'The lack of a response to the OnStar call and the fact there had been no 911 call from Marisa had also corroborated that.'

He took a sip of water. 'I know Marisa… I mean I knew her. She isn't…oh goddammit…wasn't many things but she definitely was quick on her feet.'

Something about the way he said that struck me as odd. Not the shuffle between the past and the present, but rather the reference to her not being many things. I didn't pull on that thread. His eyes were moist but his face was taut. It was a valiant effort to avert a breakdown and he barely succeeded.

I gave him a minute before I said, 'Courage almost always comes in small steps, Sam, and what you did was very brave.'

He nodded slightly. 'Since it was his first day back from vacation, the sheriff hadn't had the chance to pull out the report his officers had put together. He asked me to come back later to have a final look at it.'

As he was leaving, he turned around and said, 'Oh! I almost forgot. I decided to follow your suggestion. I'm taking the vacation after all—starting the long weekend after our next session.'

I was glad he was trying to get some answers. It had given

him the sense of purpose he needed and I was positive it was good for him. 'That sounds fantastic,' I said. 'Tell me all about it next time?'

'Sure.' He smiled faintly and was off.

◆

At our next session, Sam walked in, more upbeat than usual.

I suspected his mood had something to do with his travel plans. 'You look excited—is it because of your upcoming vacation?'

He had a timbre to his voice I had only heard when he talked about Will. 'Oh yeah! I am. I took your advice and asked John. And it's more than just a vacation—it's a cycling trip really. We have both wanted to do this trip for a long time and are really stoked about it. We're going for almost a couple of weeks and have a bunch of other fun stuff planned too.'

He was wearing shorts for the first time and he did have the calves of a cyclist. I could see the tan lines on his wrists and close to his ankles. I was happy for him and I told him so. I felt it more appropriate to let him bring up the police report when he was ready.

And he did. 'Which reminds me, I went to see the sheriff.' He paused. 'And on the way…I stopped at the site again.' I flinched when he said it.

He must have noticed my reaction. 'Don't worry, I didn't pass out this time!' He smiled and then said, 'This is embarrassing…'

Why is he embarrassed? I thought. I was the one feeling flushed because he had caught me flinching.

He continued. 'I wanted to clean it up…get rid of all the glass.'

'That is so thoughtful of you.' I said, adding, 'There's no need to be embarrassed.'

'I wasn't sure if it was okay and where I would park, so I called Matthews to check with him. He's just been super— really great guy—he sent over an officer to watch over me. He stayed there the whole time and accompanied me back to the station too.'

'I also…' he stopped mid-sentence, 'Never mind,' and dismissed the thought with a slight wave of his hand.

'No! Never, never mind!' I retorted.

He laughed before continuing. 'I don't know if I told you, but I like gardening. And baking…but that's kind of irrelevant. Anyway, I have somewhat of a green thumb and Will used to love helping out in the yard. So…I cleared out a patch at the site and planted some of his favourite flowers… I took the saplings from my yard. It felt really good. I think they might already be in blossom by the time I get back from my holiday.'

I knew he was caring but hadn't seen this sensitive side before. I had mostly seen just the anger and the frustration. I figured I had been right about him not having had the chance to express his feelings in a safe environment. I don't know why, but in that moment, I felt the need to stop my own emotions from brimming over. And I did.

◆

He sighed deeply. 'The trip to the station, however, was a totally different story,' he said in a softer and slower tone. 'They didn't have much else to report. They had checked the car for flats, malfunctions, and any signs of an accident but there hadn't been any. They had also checked the vicinity for injured animals and any related reports, *pero nada.*'

Before she had left, Lily's Spanish babble had permeated enough for me to know he had just said 'but nothing'. *I didn't know he spoke Spanish.*

'They had found the point at which the car had swerved off the embankment…from the skid marks.' He finally took a deep breath and shook his head, 'What I don't understand is…if there wasn't an accident…then why did she hit the brakes…so late?' He was looking above me, into the distance. 'The sheriff said a passer-by had called in the accident, but the lead had ended there.'

He stiffened and looked back at me. 'What did he mean by the "lead had ended there"? They are the bloody police! I asked them what they had or were planning to do about it, and they just looked at each other,' he said shrugging. 'Matthews finally explained the call had come in after the OnStar report and had therefore been logged but not reported. The call had been made from a public telephone and the caller had disconnected abruptly.'

His shoulders slumped. 'I was upset but didn't say anything because he's been a gem—Matthews, he really has. But I do feel… I need to somehow find out more…'

For the first time in a couple of months, I had seen some of the anger resurface. But I empathized with his frustration at not being able to get better answers.

He leaned back in the couch but maintained eye contact. 'The other day, when you said it was okay to be a little crazy— what did you really mean by that?'

His segue caught me off guard. 'Not sure what you're asking me, Sam.'

'I think I need to get to the bottom of this…but I'm afraid all of this…that I'm doing…might be…well…' He broke out the

91

jazz hands and shook his head in tempo. '…aahh…a little crazy.'

I didn't see why his need to get more answers was at all crazy. I thought it was time to bring out James's metaphor. 'I don't think so. What you're doing right now is trying to get the answers you need. True healing can only be complete once you have them. There's nothing crazy about that.'

'Hmm! You do make a good point, but how can I be certain it's not hurting…'

I needed to allay his concerns, so I interrupted him. 'You're just asking people to step up and do what is required—their jobs. There's no question of hurting anyone.'

He raised his hand to his mouth and bit on the side of his index finger. 'That does make sense.'

The offbeat culmination to our session gnawed at me, but something else had started niggling even more. I had begun to realize that Sam only expressed how much he missed William, but not Marisa. Even when I tried to bring Marisa into the conversation, he would drift back to Will. I wondered if this was deliberate or subconscious. Either way, I was concerned he might be repressing emotions that would hit him later.

◆

Sam skipped a few weeks after he got back from vacation because he got caught up with work. When he kept his next appointment, I was surprised to see him walk into my office holding a bunch of flowers. 'These are for you,' he said, with a smile.

I would have been happy simply with the smile. 'Oh my! They are beautiful. Thank you… Any special occasion?' I asked.

'These are the flowers I told you about last time—the ones I had planted—Will's favourite actually,' he said, laughing, I assumed, at my vain attempt to locate a vase.

'Of course I remember—they are gorgeous! He had good taste,' I said and promised to take them home and put them in a vase. 'I hope they'll last for a while—Lily's going to be back soon and I bet she'll love them too.'

'Lily? That's your daughter right, the one in all the pictures?' he pointed to my desk.

'Mm...hmm... She's been on vacation for almost ten weeks,' I replied. I resisted talking more about her because I wanted to be sensitive to his circumstances, so I continued on a tangent. 'Talking about vacations, how was yours? Tell me everything!'

He perked up. 'We had a great time—it was an adrenaline-packed vacation. We rode a lot, and I do mean a lot.' He had done his first tandem skydive and had even gotten a tattoo, which he proudly showed me. It was an elaborate and beautiful piece of Māori art that covered his entire right shoulder. 'I think the only downer was our accident, and that too, on our last day of riding. Both John and I now have our battle wounds—I on my other shoulder and he on his leg. He got it much worse than I did but he'll survive. Hey! Neither one of us was complaining though—at least it wasn't an accident while skydiving!' We both laughed. He sounded happy and I felt his excitement.

I could feel little else but happy anyhow—Lily was going to be back soon. 'Wow! That was quite an awesome vacation by the sound of it. Skydiving, eh? What was that like?'

He bounced on the couch and waved his arms, happily for a change. 'Oh! It was spectacular. Nothing quite like it. I've decided to take it up seriously, starting with weekend classes, but I'm going for my first class right after our session. Now that's doing something crazy, eh?'

He was living on the edge and I understood his need. 'It

is!' I said, 'And it sounds super fun too.'

Towards the end of our session, he brought up Lily again. 'Tell me about Lily. How old is she?'

'She's going on seventeen now,' I said.

He knit his brow. 'Isn't she in college then?'

I was surprised at how quickly he connected the dots—he did strike me as a very intelligent man. I told him she had decided to take a year off and gain some 'life experience' as she liked to call it.

He laughed. 'Kids are lucky these days. Where's she travelling? With a boyfriend?'

'No! Thank god for that—with a close friend actually.' I must have kept talking for at least a few minutes before I realized I had lost him. It was exactly what I was afraid would happen if we stuck to that topic. When I looked at him, his eyes were already glazed over and he was looking right past me.

I had to pull him back. 'Sam!' I got nothing. 'Sam!'

He snapped out of it. 'I'm sorry. I just got reminded of... Will... I'm so sorry...'

'It's okay, Sam. It really is. Their memories can never be erased.'

He shot up from the couch. 'Yes. And besides, you said I don't have to be sorry. And now, you must wish me luck.'

I knew he was referring to his first skydiving class so I didn't feel the need to ask. 'Good luck! Break a leg...or not... in this case.'

He laughed. And then, he was out in a flash.

Even though I had been able to get him to laugh, I was disappointed at the contrast between the note on which he had entered and that on which he had left. But I know better—such are the vicissitudes of bereavement. My concern about him repressing memories of Marisa continued to gnaw at me—I

94

made a note to address it explicitly. Although, it wasn't like I hadn't been trying to.

◆

I walked back to the station with the flowers in my hand. *They are beautiful! I should have asked what they're called.*

Lily and I had talked on the phone a few times—enough for me to know she was doing well and having a great time. I had called her the first few weeks but after my email, she had started reciprocating. I had been so overwhelmed when she had called first that any other thoughts, including those of the email, had been expunged from my brain. However, on a subsequent call I had asked her if she had read it, because I had not received a reply. After a brief moment of silence, she had softly said she had read it, thanked me for it, and told me she didn't want to talk about it any more. I had respected that and had been too happy about her subtle change of behaviour to care about anything else.

I continued smiling. It may also have had something to do with another first date later in the evening. The previous one hadn't worked out so well. This one was with Ryan and had been set up by a common friend. I had been told I had met him at a party before, but I couldn't put a face to the name. I did feel warmly about Ryan though, perhaps because a good friend had set up the date, which was more in line with my old school ways. I felt I was ready to believe in love again.

◆

Truce

It was finally the day of Lily's return and I was counting down the seconds. I woke up early, all ready to cook, clean, shop and mop, to get everything ready in time. She was arriving a few days before her birthday and I knew exactly what to get for her. I sifted through the mail as I started my day with a freshly brewed cup of coffee. My gaze fell on a thick, weathered, brown envelope covered with so many stamps that it was difficult to tell who it was from. I squealed in delight as I recognized the writing and realized it was from Lily. First, I ripped it open quickly, and then, it ripped me open—slowly.

Hola madre,

Cómo estás? (How are you?) I'm doing super here. Joanna and I had a great time together—we started in Madrid and after travelling through Seville, Malaga, and Valencia, we ended back in Barcelona. It's a beautiful country with beautiful people and the weather has been absolutely gorgeous! The food, the

beaches, and the architecture have all been
spectacular as well. You would have loved
it here. Perhaps some day, we can come
back together and I can show you around.

My heart was melting and I read slowly, allowing my soul to
steep in each and every word. She proceeded to tell me the
highlights of all the places they had visited, accompanied by
meticulously numbered pictures. *The stamps must have cost her
a fortune,* I thought.

Barcelona, without even a shadow of a doubt,
has been the best. Our first day here, both
of us wanted to see the opera, but these
are the kinds of things where planning would
have helped. By the time we got there,
tickets for the entire season had already
been sold out—all but the most expensive
ones. Come to think of it, we could have
sacrificed Joanna!

I laughed out loudly.

We were naturally bummed, so we decided to
drown our sorrows in…well, you don't need
to know that.
    All you need to know is, I think folks
over here are way cooler than they are
back over there, in the little village we
like to call 'developed'!
    Later in the evening, walking through
the streets, lo and behold, what do we
see? You better believe it—a live opera,

97

TRUCE

tucked away between some medieval buildings, in the backstreets of Barcelona. It was a free street-performance by some up-and-coming artists. It was the most magical night under the stars ever and no one got sacrificed! You must remind me to show you the videos when I'm back.

She went on to talk about the culture, the food, especially at the 'mercados', and then she switched to our strongest, common love, besides ice cream of course.

I'm now officially in love with Gaudí. You are right—he was a genius. If you track his work through the years, you can almost see him learning and his techniques evolving. And that is what I have been doing since Joanna left. She found him 'gaudy'—she thought it was funny. I thought she was safer leaving!

Each of his creations is a marvel, yet in some ways, Park Güell, La Sagrada Família, and Casa Batlló bring the best of his distinctiveness together.

My favourite however, for many reasons, is Casa Batlló. In my opinion, this is where he brought the best of what he had to offer in construction as well as in design—and with a flourish not seen in some of his other works. It has inspired me enough to make it the subject of my paper.

I know I get this passion from you and from the hundreds of books ornamenting our

lives, but it's really quite something else
to be able to see all of this first-hand.
I hope you enjoy all the pictures I took
for you—they're a small thank you for all
your support in making this possible.

I was thrilled she was enjoying her love for architecture. Secretly, I hoped our common love would help us build our relationship anew.

I have also found a part-time job now,
ironically as an usher at the opera house—so
it's free opera for me every night. And it
gives me a lot of time during most days to
soak in more of Gaudí and to meet like-
minded people at walking tours and meet-
ups. When I'm tired of doing that, I find
myself a nice and quiet cafe overlooking
one of his buildings to work on my paper
and college applications.

I was glad she had started thinking about college and next steps too. And then, out of the blue, she launched right into it. A new page, at least, might have prepared me better.

I've been thinking about what you told me
the day I was leaving. I tried to forget
it but couldn't. And then your email brought
it up again. In some ways, I'm glad it
did. Had it not been for your email, I
may have never had the idea or the courage
to write my own thoughts down on paper.
    Until that day, when you saw him punishing

me the way he used to, only I know how
many times I had wanted to talk to you
about it but kept chickening out. And then,
things happened so fast. You called the
police and kicked him out, and then the
divorce. I know now that I owe you a big
thank you for coming to my rescue as soon
as you found out.

That day wasn't the first time it had
happened. The first time had been after my
thirteenth birthday. I don't know if you
remember, but I think he was out of work
again and had been spending a lot of time
at home.

Of course I remembered. He had difficulty holding on to a job,
mostly because of his anger issues, and had therefore become a
freelancer. That way, others had managed to avoid his anger, at
least at the workplace, but the stream of projects hadn't always
been steady.

I continued reading.

You were at work when I got back from
school. He was sitting with his back to
the door and I hugged him from behind.
It caused him to spill his drink on some
papers and he just spun around and slapped
me. I've tried my best to blot out the
memories from that day but I think I had
started crying. The more I cried, the more
he punished me. It seemed like he gave up
only when he couldn't have dished out any

100

more! He just picked me up, threw me on the couch, and left.

I must have fallen asleep because the next things I remember are his finger pointing in my face and threats of doing worse if I told you or anyone else. I had tried forgetting it and may have succeeded to an extent as well. Which is when it happened for the second time, and then another. Each time, not only did the beating grow worse but also the threats. Sometimes he would tell me you knew, and at others he would tell me it would be worse for you if I told on him.

Each time it happened, I thought of telling you, but I didn't know if I was more afraid for myself or for you. I feel my biggest fear was that I would find out you knew and weren't doing anything about it. That would have killed me.

By this time my tears were pouring, blotting the ink on the paper. I had to stop reading. It was a while before I had the strength to pick up the letter again.

Now that I know more and can think calmly, I realize his behaviour had to do with his anger issues and his drinking problem. It doesn't make it easier for me to understand or accept. Although, I do understand now why he would always only beat me on my back. It was so that no one ever found

out. The only person who ever found out
was Roy, but he had said something like
'So what? My dad hits me all the time
too,' and it became even more difficult for
me to share with anyone else.

I remembered all the meal times—she would prefer standing
around the island rather than sitting, and the grief I gave her
because of it. My pain had cascaded into anger by then and I
was fuming. It took immense effort to finish reading the letter.

It has taken me a long time to finally
share this with you, and I feel, almost
as long to write this letter! But I'm glad
both our stories are out in the open now—I
think we've both been through enough. And
after all, he should be the common enemy
and not you or I. I'm still trying to figure
all this out, but at least I understand a
whole lot more—so thank you for sharing.

I miss you. I hope you get this letter
in time and that we can try and do better
when I return.

xoxo,
Lily

◆

My state of emotional turmoil must have lasted for a long time
because by the time I resurfaced it was way past noon and my
stomach was growling. But it didn't matter. I was still in a daze

when it was time to pick her up from the airport. I was not the only one excited about her return. Joanna was too, and she had wanted to come with me to the airport to surprise Lily. On the one hand, the mother in me didn't want to share her daughter with anyone else, but on the other hand, the friend didn't want to deprive her of her hopeful BFF either. The friend kept winning—no contest! To be honest, I was also glad Lily had found a good friend in Joanna—one she was unwilling to sacrifice, even for the opera.

It was when Joanna rang the doorbell that my daze was finally broken. She was wearing a beautiful blue dress and had her gorgeous golden hair neatly tied in pigtails. It had already begun to get chilly outside and she was wearing a denim jacket, which complemented her dress rather well. I was afraid that next to her my Lily would look like a leprechaun.

On the drive over, all Joanna could talk of was how excited she was about Lily's return and how much she was enjoying her studies at the Fashion Institute of Technology. She had enrolled in a bachelor's degree programme in fashion design, and loved being in the city and her classmates as well. I was trying to listen to her as best as I could and ask her at least remotely relevant questions, but most of the drive was still a blur. I was overwhelmed by excitement, wondering about the letter's significance to our relationship. *Had she granted me amnesty and was ready to move on? Was it the declaration of a truce and were we friends, finally?* I felt bolstered to continue doing the work that needed to be done to salvage the most important relationship of my life.

The tearful hugs at the airport reflected my state of mind, although I was the only one crying. Both of them were laughing and chirping like birds in a tree. They were just the two of them—from the sounds of it, however, it was as if they were roosting in the hundreds. Other than the difference in their attires and the colour of their hair, they could have very easily passed off as sisters.

Once we were in the car and the cacophony had dissipated for a minute, she put a hand on mine and said, 'I missed you, Cynthia.'

'Me too, dear,' I beamed back.

And then they were off again.

I was focusing on the exits out of the airport, when I heard them speaking surreptitiously in their coded P-language before breaking out into impish laughter. In my imagination, Joanna had asked her why I was crying so much, and Lily had replied with something funny, which my imagination didn't want to fathom. *Are we back to business as usual? At least, it didn't sound like an insult.* I couldn't care less, because my gorgeous golliwog was back in my nest.

◆

Joanna helped us unload the suitcases and carry them in, and we all had tea and cake around the island. Lily sounded excited to be back and was recounting all her fun experiences. It was apparent a lot of them were being censored for my benefit. It was pretty late by the time Joanna left. Lily said she was jet-lagged and was going to turn in as well.

She was halfway up the staircase when, without looking back, she said, 'Pretty flowers! Who are they from?'

I glanced over at the flowers Sam had given me a few days back—they had found their home in a crystal vase right at the centre of the counter. 'Oh those? Umm...'

Without waiting, she asked, 'What are they called?'

I was still struggling to come up with an intelligible response, but it didn't matter because she was already inside her bedroom. Then her music started and drowned out my thoughts and everything... *Everything that is not evil in this world.*

◆

Coincidence

It was Lily's seventeenth birthday. Joanna had dragged her out on some pretext, but it was really for a surprise lunch with friends. I knew because I had helped Joanna plan it. Lily was going to be back soon though, and we had decided to reinstate our annual birthday-ice-cream-blowout ritual. I was sitting on the bed wrapping her gift when I heard the buzzing of my cell phone. Trying to keep the wrapping paper from misbehaving, I took the call without checking who it was from.

'Hello!' I said. Silence. 'Hello!' I repeated, followed by, 'Who's this?'

The voice was sniffling. 'Cynthia… This is…Sam.'

'Sam!' I said, trying to tone down the surprise. I was surprised, less because it was him, but more because of how he sounded. 'What happened? Are you okay?'

'No, not really… I think I'm having a breakdown. I…I need to see you.'

He had been improving steadily but had missed a couple of sessions. *This sounds like an unexpected and pronounced regression,* I thought. 'Uh…' I didn't know what to say. Although I did see patients at home, I didn't want anything to ruin my plans with Lily. The wrapping paper renewed its bid to escape.

I was about to protest, but he spoke again. 'Not for too long…just briefly… I really need to speak to you. You had promised to be available, remember?'

I found it upsetting that he was throwing my offer of being available to talk in my face at a time like that. 'I understand you need to talk, but can you at least tell me what happened?' I asked, partly with the intent of finding out more and partly as a delaying tactic.

He sputtered more than usual. 'I'm…just…afraid…'

I gave him a few seconds to complete his sentence, but he had clearly trailed off. 'I understand, Sam—this has been really tough on you. It's just that I'm home and have some important plans… Perhaps we can talk now on…'

He didn't let me finish. 'No, no, no, Cynthia! You don't understand. I'm afraid I might be going a little crazy and I need to see you in person.'

I was concerned but I was sure I could help him by talking over the phone.

'I really need just a few minutes… I won't take too much time. I'm driving around anyway and can be there in less than fifteen minutes… Please…'

Many of my patients know where I live. So did he, since he had dropped me home some time back. But at that moment I felt strangely vulnerable. I knew Lily would be back soon. I made a last-ditch effort. 'I feel your pain, but could we at least try…'

There were sounds of fresh sobs. 'It's his birthday today… and I just need your help to get me over this…'

He kept speaking but I was in shock. I couldn't believe the

coincidence. I remembered one of our initial sessions when he had talked about Will's birthday for the first time. Something had struck me about the timing, but there had been way too many other emotional stimuli to focus on.

'Cynthia? Are you there?'

'Yes, yes! Oh, I didn't realize it was his birthday, Sam. I'm so sorry.' I was too dumbfounded to say anything else but, 'Sure...sure... Come on over.'

I had just about enough time to finish wrapping, change, and look at my notes from our previous session. I had decided to do a Marisa-intervention but, clearly, this was not going to be the day for that.

◆

When he plodded in with drooping shoulders, I was glad that I had decided to see him. He talked about Will and the things they would do for his birthday. 'I'm missing him too much and I can't get him out of my mind. The memories... The pictures... They're all haunting me...and I can't take it any more.'

I realized the significance of Will's first birthday since his passing, but I still couldn't get over the coincidence. I felt Sam's plight, yet was in self-preservation mode. I didn't want the conversation to just wade. 'When you called me you said you were afraid—what do you think you're afraid of?'

He struggled—perhaps it was the change of tempo. 'Oh! I think I've accepted my fate but all this I'm doing—trying to get answers—I'm afraid it's holding us back... I mean...'

I thought I knew what he meant—he was referring to our therapy and sessions together. He had been trying hard to get the answers he needed from the police. Perhaps the lack of answers did suggest there really weren't any, and it was going to be up to him to get closure. I stopped him from explaining further and encouraged him to move on. I also wanted to encourage him, more subtly of course, to leave.

He was nodding, slowly, yet consistently. 'Hmm…I think you're right… Perhaps that's what's best now…' I felt relieved, for both of us. Then he made a switchback. 'I've been on the phone with my family all day—thinking I can move on but it hasn't helped. I miss him…and I want to do right by him.'

I had fought my way back into my daughter's life and needed to be on top of my game with her. In the session with Sam, however, I was about to hit rock-bottom. I found it increasingly awkward that he didn't talk about his wife as much. In a completely blithe lapse of reason, I blurted, 'Don't you miss Marisa too?'

He stared squarely at me. 'What do you mean? Of course I do. What kind of a question is that?'

I had barely started explaining, 'It's just that…' when he cut me off, which was okay because I had no idea what the end of my sentence was going to be anyway.

He was clutching both armrests of the chair and his knuckles had turned white. 'Just what, Cynthia? Have you ever stopped to consider how you might feel if it ever came to a choice between your daughter and…' He stopped himself.

But it was too late. He had already touched a raw nerve. I was seething inside and had to tell myself, *He doesn't know, Cynthia… If only he did…he wouldn't have dared…* I had to really focus to keep my breathing normal. I find that at times voicing an apology helps myself as well. 'I'm sorry—I didn't mean it the way it sounded.' But my insanity was far from over. 'When was her birthday, Sam?'

Why? Why did I just ask that? Have I completely lost it?

'What does that have to do with any of this? It was last month. Was that your way of apologizing?'

I wanted to ask how come he never talked about her? How come he didn't miss her as much? How come he didn't go through any of that on her birthday? Instead, and thankfully, what came out was, 'I'm just trying to take your mind off, Will.'

'Oh!' He coughed up a laugh. 'Well… You definitely succeeded with that.'

I knew it wasn't meant as a compliment but I reciprocated his laughter, and that diffused the situation.

Soon he was doing better, but I wasn't. Lily was going to be back any minute, so I was relieved when he thanked me before getting up to take leave.

◆

Serendipity

Sam and I were walking out of my office in the basement when we both turned sharply and I saw Lily bounding down the steps. A giant porcupine, albeit a lovable one, might have looked no different. Her heavy leather hoofs were clumping down the steps two at a time. I was sure we had a crime scene in the making, because she was hurtling right towards Sam and showing no imminent signs of stopping.

'Whooo…aaa!' she exhaled, stopping dead in her tracks on the last step. She had to arch her torso and throw her arms out in front of her, to prevent a head-on collision with Sam. 'Well, hello!' she said, catching her breath and squaring off with him with her arms akimbo.

Sam didn't even flinch. I remember being concerned about his reaction time. I also remember being a little disappointed—at least a part of me was. It was the part that would have loved to see a little gentle head-butting—to see who came out on top in the battle between porcupine Lily and prickly Sam! I remember…because later I regretted having wished for it.

'Well, hello to you too, young lady,' he said, laughing

and doffing an imaginary hat. It was like a scene from a cheesy western. I was sure the 'young lady' was his way of overcompensating for her appearance. She looked like a ghoul. Halloween was just around the corner but, then again, with her it was Halloween at home every day!

He introduced himself. 'I'm Sam. And might you be Lily?'

'That would be correct, Uncle Sam!' she retorted, shooting me a quick glance. He laughed.

'Cool outfit!' He stuck out a thumbs-up. 'Is it from that store…uh…what's its name… Hot Topic?'

Wait just a minute! How in god's name does he know that? I bet Lily was asking herself that very question.

She smiled. 'Yes! How'd ya know? Do your kids shop there too?'

Sam was caught off guard. I wanted to come to his rescue, but I was too far away on the sidelines of the surreal scene between them. He recovered just enough to be able to whisper, 'Uh, no! I don't have any kids… But if I did, he would have loved your sense of style.' His smile returned, but only just.

She looked down at me, raised her eyebrows, and said, 'See! Finally, someone who understands fashion.'

Any higher, and her nose would be touching the ceiling! I wanted to boot Sam for encouraging her.

Looking back at him, she continued, 'Hey! We were just about to step out for some ice cream. Care to join?'

What is she doing? She isn't the one in charge… Wait…it's her birthday… Maybe today she is…

He stumbled again, but asked to be rescued this time. 'Uh?' he said, looking at me questioningly.

'Why are you looking at me? She's the one inviting you,' I said.

'Sure,' he said, 'why not? Uncle Sam is a sucker when it comes to ice cream.' They both laughed. I didn't. I didn't want to share her with him, and, that too, on her birthday.

◆

His car was parked behind ours, so he offered to drive. Lily threw in her bag onto the backseat and climbed in after it. The banter continued on the way to, during, and on the way back from ice cream. Even at the ice cream parlour, I was sidelined. I chose a strawberry soft serve and was conveniently relegated to finding us a table. My ice cream had already whittled down to a smear by the time they both sat down with their ginormous portions. They claimed they had gone with completely different trimmings but I couldn't tell the difference. I was hopeful the ice cream would shut them up, but it wasn't to be.

Between mouthfuls, Lily said to Sam, 'Hey! You said you don't have kids—so then, who gave you the friendship bands?'

I wondered how he would react.

Lily, however, had other ideas. 'Oh, wait! Don't tell me. Is it your hot twenty-something-year-old girlfriend?'

I couldn't believe what she had just said. 'Lily!' I screamed, and some strawberry soft serve sprayed out.

Sam almost choked on his bite. Thankfully, it was just ice cream—even if it wasn't, I might not have cared!

He said, 'What? We thirty-something-year-olds can't exchange friendship bands?'

She refused to back down. 'Thirty-something... Ha! You're funny!'

Had it not been for his unbridled laughter, I would have exacted revenge on his behalf by smashing the last of my cone

113

into her nose! While my brain froze, and not because of the ice cream, they switched seamlessly to arguing over the trappings that went best with the already overloaded rocky road they both had chosen. *Louts*, I thought! They were clearly getting along like a house on fire. Ironically though, I was the one burning. The only other person I had seen her that chatty with, was Joanna.

◆

Almost aeons later, on the way back, he looked at her in the rear-view mirror and said, 'Your mother told me you were on a vacation. How was it?'

'Muy bien... very good,' she replied, while still looking out the window.

'Sí? Lo pasaste bien?' He shot a glance at me and then quickly followed up with, 'Did you have a good time?'

I assumed the question in English had been a translation for my benefit.

'Claro! Hablas español?' she asked.

Why is she asking him if he speaks Spanish? I don't!

Sam replied, *'Sí, un poco.'*

A little? I thought. That's much less than how annoyed I was getting, with both of them.

'Yo también,' she said.

Yes! We get you speak a little too, but what about me? How rude!

'Suficiente para que ella no entiende!' he said looking sideways at me.

Wait... What? What did he just say?

They both laughed loudly. I felt all my blood rush to my face. I was pretty sure I had turned red—and that the shade was three parts embarrassment, two of feeling left out, and one, for good measure, of my ego getting in the way of asking what the heck they were on about.

She put a hand on my shoulder and explained that he just teased me by saying that they both spoke enough Spanish for me to not understand.

He apologized. It didn't matter. *He is already in the doghouse.*

The conversation switched to her trip to Spain, in English. He asked her, 'Did you get a chance to go see Casa Batlló?'

She quipped, 'See it? I was practically living inside it!'

Sam laughed heartily. I would have joined in too, but something was niggling me. At the time, I attributed it to my annoyance at both of them getting along so well.

He said, 'Then you must have seen the video tour—my company is the one that developed it. What did you think of it?'

'Oh my god! No way!' Lily sounded ecstatic. 'It has to be the best video tour I have ever seen. First, I thought I would keep bumping into people but I was surprised when I didn't. I absolutely loved the part when the turtle comes to life from the skylight!'

She turned her attention to me. 'Cynthia! You absolutely have to see it—I have a video on my cell phone—I'll show it to you later. When you sign up for the video tour, they give you this cell phone-like device you can point at different design elements inside the house. And when you do, the video on the device brings the inspiration behind the design element to life. There's this skylight, which is clearly inspired from a turtle. When you point the device at it, the turtle in the video comes to life and swims away. It's simply breathtaking! You would love it.'

Sam also took a page out of Lily's book and addressed me. 'She's right, you would—judging by your fondness for

115

architecture and design.' He stole a quick glance at me. 'Have you been to Spain?'

It was finally my turn. 'No, and I'm sure I would love it. It's next on my list—whenever that might be.' I was thrilled Lily was as chatty as she was—she had hardly ever been like that with me, let alone in front of a stranger. I hadn't even minded her calling me by my first name…as much. *Sam, on the other hand, will have to pay with a pound of his flesh!* Luckily for him, we were almost pulling into our driveway, but I did have to get in the last word. 'Oh look! *Mi casa*!' They both laughed hysterically. I kept my poker face. I felt like my chaperone duty was finally over.

◆

We said our goodbyes on the driveway. Lily was the first to turn around and start walking in. He looked past me at her and then exclaimed, 'Wait! Why do you have a "CAD Cat" button on your bag?'

Of course, she knew he was talking to her. I didn't even know what a 'cat cat' was—that's what I had heard! I was sure I was reverting to red—the same shade as before.

She swung around like a dervish. 'You know the "CAD Cats"? But how? You're not a girl…or…is there something you're not telling us?' She smiled mischievously at him.

The girl badly needs a filter! I'm going to have to talk to her.

He laughed unabashedly. 'Yes! Very well, in fact.' He must have noticed me changing to crimson and was polite enough to explain that the 'CAD Cats' was a global organization of girls and women united by their aspiration to excel at computer-aided design.

DARK BLOSSOM

He might as well have said it in Spanish because it meant nothing to me! Lily's love for technology is something she gets from Connor—he is a graphic designer.

She walked back towards us. 'I'm a member of the Connecticut chapter. And you?'

'Well—it's a long story—my company is one of their official sponsors and we host a get together for their New York chapter at my city office every quarter. In fact, the next one should be soon—you're more than welcome to come and join, only if it's okay with your mother, of course.'

As if I'm even here! I was at a far, faraway location, trying to reassess my place in the universe, not to mention in this triangle. So I just mumbled something unintelligible, which in their secret dialect apparently translated to 'sure'.

They both sounded jubilant and, on my distant planet, I was coming to terms with my insecurities around losing my daughter to a stranger on her birthday while trying to convince myself it couldn't hurt.

Still, it had been a fun evening. I had really enjoyed myself with Lily and, unexpectedly so, with Sam too.

◆

Crossing Lines

The next day, I had little choice but to turn part-private eye and dig up everything I could on Sam's company and the 'caddy cats'. I had to make an informed decision on whether or not to let my daughter go to his event.

It took me a while on Google to first get the names of his company and that of the 'CAD Cats' right, and then to get the lowdown. Everything looked legit and I couldn't come up with any loopholes. That Sam was a patient was the only thing I could come up with.

I would make a lousy private eye, I thought.

After some intricate negotiations, Lily and I reached a compromise. On the evening of the event, she would let me drop her off at Sam's office and would come straight back to mine after, so we could return home together. As it turned out, Sam's office was not too far from mine, which was convenient— logistically, not emotionally.

◆

On the day of the event, Lily couldn't contain her excitement.

She rushed as we walked to Sam's office, which was just as well since it kept me warm. After dropping her off, I returned to my own office, more slowly. I turned the heat all the way up and settled down for an evening of catching up on some reading. I found my attention wavering. Before I knew it I was pacing up and down in the pigeonhole I call an office, waiting as patiently as I possibly could for her to return. I even had to turn the heat off.

I stopped pacing only after Lily called and said she was waiting downstairs. She sounded ecstatic and was smiling ear to ear. Throughout the train ride back home, all she could talk about was Sam-this and 'CAD Cats'-that. Sam ran a successful tech firm and their CAD software was very popular with architects. The company provided the 'CAD Cats' a free licence to their software in exchange for product feedback and promotion. It was a win-win for both and the get together was a regular event to foster the alliance. She had not only met some of her friends who were members of the Connecticut chapter, but also made some new acquaintances from New York. My concerns had been adequately allayed too, given I could connect the dots better. I think that might have been her plan all along. She talked feverishly all the way back home and then all the way through dinner as well. She didn't have much of an appetite as she had already eaten enough hors d'oeuvres at the event, yet she gave me company—a first in recent memory. I was grateful for it and happy on my island.

She even helped me put things away, and by then I was almost smug, thinking that things between us were all hunky-dory. So complacent in fact, that I didn't even see it coming. She had set up the play to perfection—she had driven to the basket, drawn my defences down, and was about to dish the perfect layup. She put her elbows on the island, propped her chin on her palms, looked at me doe-eyed, and said, 'Oh! By the way—he offered me an internship.'

'What? Why? When?' was the most coherent response I could emit.

Then she started walking away. She must have predicted my response. 'Don't worry. You can ask him all your questions yourself, because I invited him over for dinner this weekend.'

What? Why? When? I thought these questions inside my head, lest I came across as an adult with an IQ of twenty.

I was feeling naive and exposed, and she was already halfway up the stairs. I had to bring my defences back up and protest, somehow. 'But…'

She interrupted. 'I figured you'd want to spend some time getting to know my future boss.'

'Uh! Ah! Right…' I uttered. *She only looks like a porcupine, but she is really a wily fox!*

She delivered the coup de grâce. 'Well, you better get to it, Cynthia, because he's expecting an invitation from you soon.' Then she was gone and soon her music stampeded over everything else.

I had braced myself for the ignominy of a layup, but that was a monster jam!

I was too shocked to do anything about it that night. I thought I'd prepare my comeback for the next day. I had planned to take a romance novel I had been meaning to finish to bed that night, but the only things that crept into the covers were my thoughts of Lily and, of all people, Sam. *What kind of conflict did this situation present?* On the one hand, he had been doing much better and I didn't know how long he'd still be my patient, but on the other hand, I had been hoping for him to continue so we could explore a few more issues for his benefit.

I must have fallen asleep thinking how happy she was,

because when I woke up I wasn't as averse to having him over for dinner.

◆

Later that afternoon, I sent him a text. 'Hi Sam! Hope you're well. Thanks for having Lily over yesterday. She had a great time.'

He replied, 'Yeah! She's a terrific kid. It was a fun evening for everyone. You're both welcome.'

I followed up. 'Would love to have you over for dinner at our place—this weekend if it works for you?'

'It works perfectly. Delighted to, in fact. Thanks!'

And just like that, he went from being my wounded patient to my delighted guest.

◆

Metamorphosis

Lily was as excited about the dinner as she had been for the event at Sam's office. Unbeknown to me, she had decided to go shopping for the evening. I didn't feel gypped when I found out she had gone with Joanna—I couldn't have picked a better companion myself. While shopping, Lily sent me a few messages with pictures of clothes she was trying on. I was ecstatic. It was a new high for our relationship.

On the day of the dinner, Lily helped set and prepare the menu. She was a bundle of energy. I, on the other hand, was a bit nervous and couldn't quite put a finger on the reason. *Good god, woman*—I thought to myself—*You're a psychologist! This is the kind of stuff you should be able to figure out by yourself.* Discovering I was talking to myself didn't help matters.

◆

Lily was still upstairs getting ready when the doorbell rang. I greeted him at the door and he walked in with a small bouquet of lilies in one hand and a nicely wrapped package in the other. The lilies were orange—I wondered if he knew it was my favourite colour.

He was looking nice—he had still kept his beard but it was well-groomed, as was his hair—I complimented him. We wavered between a hello with a handshake and a hug with a peck on the cheek, to which he said, 'And I thought this would be socially awkward.' We both burst out laughing, which cut through the tension. He handed me the flowers. 'These are for you. I figured they're your favourite.'

I laughed. 'Cute, Sam…cute! So what do you have in the other hand—the moon?'

I heard a 'huh?'. I don't think he got my reference to the fact that I'm named after the Greek goddess of the moon. I didn't feel the need to explain either. *Ha! I'll get back at you yet, buster…for colluding with my daughter in Spanish.*

'Lily is still getting ready. Come right in, won't you?' I said, waving for him to follow.

He offered another icebreaker. 'Beautiful place you've got here. Couldn't quite tell from the dungeon…err…I mean the basement the other day!'

Is he trying to be funny? I don't think he understands the notion very well. I shot over my shoulder, 'You do realize I'm going to be serving you dinner very soon, right?'

I didn't look back but I was confident I had shut him up.

At the island, I served us wine. We had just about taken our first sips when I heard a sharp reprimand from the stairs. It was Lily. 'Aren't you gonna wait for me? How impolite!'

She continued her walk down. I think god may have intervened in that moment—to prevent the wine from erupting through my nose. Even though I had offered her advice as best as I could, I wasn't sure exactly what she had picked up during her shopping spree. She was wearing a light-grey turtleneck and a navy blue, knee-length skirt—her tresses had been tamed with the help of a headband too. She was looking like a tycoon. Well, not really, but compared to the tyke she usually dressed up as, she was. I was staring at her with my mouth agape as she floated to the island and nonchalantly poured herself a small glass of wine. *What else had she picked up in Europe?*

He complimented her. I think. 'Wow! Lily, Is that you?'

'I know!' I echoed mischievously. 'What did you do with my daughter?'

'Whaaat?' she drawled, as if the answer should have been obvious. 'I'm hoping to get a job tonight.'

'I'll drink to that.' Sam said and proposed a toast, 'To employment!'

'Since when did you start drinking, young lady?' I asked. Without waiting for a response, I said, 'Actually, on second thought, don't answer that.' Sam was the only one who laughed.

But she likes getting in the last word—she takes after her mother. 'In Spain. They're way cooler over there. I think we can be prudes here sometimes. I'm so glad you're not like that… er…Mother!'

I knew she had autocorrected from 'Cynthia' to 'Mother' because of Sam. *Did she just wink at him?*

'Oh yes! Your trip to Spain,' Sam said. 'Tell me more about it. It's quite possibly my favourite place in the world.'

She started talking about her trip animatedly and I got busy serving dinner at the island. Somewhere through dinner, he asked Lily about her plans for college. She told him she had already applied to a few schools of architecture and was waiting to hear back from them. She was hoping to be accepted by her 'first choice' and pursue an internship with Sam until next fall.

I was surprised that she had said 'first choice'. *Shouldn't she have just said NYU?* I thought we had talked about her staying local.

That's when he remembered his other package. 'Oh! Which reminds me—' he said, putting his glass down, 'I got something for you.' He handed over the nicely wrapped package to her.

'Thank you,' Lily said. 'Can I open it?'

'Absolutely! It's for you,' he said, raising his glass in her direction.

She ripped it open. It was a book but it was upside down. She flipped it over and started laughing. He followed.

Why am I not getting it? 'What's funny?' I asked.

Lily paused to explain. 'It's… Ha! Ha! An instruction manual for the software his company develops.'

And then they both started laughing again.

Oh my god! They're both nerds!

'Ha! Ha! Does that mean the job is mine?' she asked.

'Like I told you, that depends on your mother.' He then looked at me. 'I'm sorry, by the way—didn't mean to encroach. I just figured it would, be good for her.'

I wanted to feel relevant, if not useful. 'What will she be doing there?'

'Well…that kind of depends on her. We usually have at least half a dozen interns at any given time. They do all kinds of jobs—test the product, help the engineers with development, and even make sales calls. Most of them are between seventeen and twenty-three, so she should fit right in.'

Lily chimed in as well. 'And they're all really nice. Not just the interns—everybody really is.'

I raised my glass to take a sip. 'It's really up to you, dear—you're a grown young woman now, clearly.'

She dropped her fork with a splatter and jumped off the counter-stool to hug me. 'Thank you! Thank you!'

I couldn't remember the last time we were so happy—either on my island or off it.

◆

Secret

The conversation caromed jovially around a range of topics. When it returned to her internship, she looked at Sam and said, 'Oh! Are you going to be my boss? Does that mean I can't call you Uncle Sam any more?'

Sam guffawed.

She continued, 'Hmm... Maybe for the last time then. So, Uncle Sam, tell me—what do you do with my mother? I mean...you don't have any...' she started ticking her head to one side and stammering, pretending to have a fit, 'g... g... going on...'

Sam almost choked with laughter.

'Lily!' I screamed. I was mortified.

She said, 'Whaaat? I'm sorry—he looks normal to me.' She pointed her open palm in his direction, while grinning at me.

I had little choice but to apologize for her. 'I'm so sorry Sam—I have no control over her.' I proceeded to take the glass of wine away from her. 'And that's the end of that.'

'It's all right,' he said. 'I've been struggling with a personal crisis... I lost someone very dear to me and talking to your mother helps…a lot.'

Again, with the 'someone', I thought. Why just some…one?

Lily was much more considerate then. 'Oh! I didn't realize. I'm sorry.'

'It's okay. It's been a while…just over a year in…' He broke off mid-sentence and just looked blankly at Lily. He shook his head to break the spell. 'Uh! But I'm doing much better now, thanks to her,' he said, tilting his head in my direction.

'And what do you talk about?' Somehow, she had managed to get her paws back on the glass and was licking the last sip from it.

Sam's voice had become softer. 'I tell her about things that happened and how they made me feel…and she helps me understand my feelings better.'

It's a reasonable explanation.

He continued stumbling. 'And then there are times…when we talk about stuff…which helps me…unlock secrets…that I keep, even from myself. And that helps me deal with them better. She's pretty good at it.'

Lily looked at me wide-eyed, and I had to check myself from blushing overtly. She said, 'Oooh! I'm really scared now.' Then she stiffened and looked straight ahead. 'I have some deep secrets too.'

Sam was oblivious to the change in her demeanour. 'Yeah? But if your mom knows, then they're really not…' He couldn't get to the end of his sentence.

'No! Even from her, I mean.' She had stopped eating and was twirling her hair around her finger—something I hadn't seen her do since she had fallen into the 'Roy Band' and started dressing like a ghoul. I had to pinch myself to remind me she was indeed my own daughter!

128

He was still oblivious. 'Then I wouldn't look her in the eyes and say that,' he teased. 'All kids your age have to have…'

She interrupted him again. 'Not kiddie stuff. Important ones.'

What secret is she talking about now? I thought we had told each other everything. There was clearly more to it than I knew. I was a little concerned but didn't want to put her on the spot.

He finally noticed how grave she looked and his tone changed. 'All kids have secrets—as they must—it's part of their identity. My suh…' He choked up. He wasn't ready to talk about the loss of his family in front of Lily. He cleared his throat and began again. 'When I was a kid about your age, I had a lot of secrets from my parents too. I was afraid to share them, but keeping them inside used to give me nightmares. Then, one day, when I couldn't take the nightmares any more, I told them everything. They were very supportive and helped me figure stuff out and, best of all, I stopped getting the nightmares.'

That was well handled, Sam. He is good with her, I found myself thinking. I wasn't sure how much I liked the idea, but it was good for her too.

Lily, on the other hand, wasn't so convinced. 'Hmm… But… Maybe…'

Sam continued looking at Lily. 'Perhaps you and I should trade? I still have secrets.'

Lily laughed. I was looking at her but felt like he had shot a glance in my direction. I looked to check, but either it was my imagination or he had already turned his gaze back at her.

They were looking at each other, but I felt they were really staring into space. *Am I the only one not living a double life?*

Lily broke the standoff. 'Naah! They wouldn't interest you.' She added, 'But the big secret of tonight should. I baked a pie!

Should we have dessert?'

'Sure!' Sam and I said in unison.

The dessert was good, really good. She baked well if she had a recipe to follow, but her cooking was a separate matter altogether! I remembered him mentioning he baked too. I wanted to bring it up but I was distracted. After dessert, he helped clean up. Then Lily and I walked with him to the driveway to wish him goodbye.

He went first. 'Thanks! Really! It was a fun evening. And the dinner and dessert—both three Michelin stars!'

He wasn't done. 'Here's an idea—I'm having a get together at my place, next month on the sixteenth. Why don't you both come? It'll mostly be colleagues from office and their families. In fact, Lily even met a few of them the other day.'

'Sure!' Lily said.

I had to take matters into my own hands. 'That's really sweet of you. Mind if we confirm in a couple of days?'

'Of course—take your time,' he said and then turned to Lily. 'Young lady, welcome aboard,' he said shaking her hand. Then he reached over and gave me a hug. 'Thank you!'

It felt more like a wrap and caught me off guard. 'Oh! Of course! See you soon.'

◆

As we walked back in, Lily followed slowly and kicked a tiny pebble out of her way. I asked, 'Everything okay, dear? Anything you'd like to talk about?'

Without looking at me, she said softly, 'Maybe…but not now… I'm too tired.'

We hadn't really been able to speak about the letter, and I

wondered if that was what she had on her mind. Over dinner, it had sounded serious. *I hope everything's okay. I'm really not as good at extracting secrets as Sam made me out to be—not with Lily anyway.*

On her way up the stairs, she stopped, turned around, looked at me, and said, 'He's nice… Thanks, Cynthia.'

◆

Back in the comfort of my bedroom, I felt a little niggle and wanted to make sure Sam had reached home.

I typed out a text to him. 'Hey! Thanks for coming over. It was a fun evening indeed. Have you reached?'

But I didn't send it—for quite a few minutes. Then, I hit delete a few times. And sent a different one instead. 'Hey! Thanks for coming over. It was a fun evening indeed. The gifts were very thoughtful.' I added a smiley at the end of it.

He replied a few minutes later. 'Glad you liked them. See you soon.'

◆

Fledgling's Flight

I had decided not to broach the subject of the secret with Lily. She had to come to terms with being able to trust me in her own time. Besides, she was occupied with the internship. She kept busy when she got back home and was spending all her free time with her new friends from work. She was having a good time and I didn't want to come in the way. Even during dinner on most days, she'd either be catching up with work or reading some magazine on architecture.

One evening at dinner, I asked, 'How's the internship coming along, dear?'

Without looking up from her folder and without stopping to chew her fodder, she replied, 'Great!'

Great! That's it?

But I wasn't about to give up so easily. 'How're the people over there?'

She timed her response between two mouthfuls. 'Awesome! Everybody's real nice.'

Perhaps I should run her under hot water. It might help.

I'm stubborn too. I counted down from ten. 'What're you

working on over there?'

She stopped reading.

I weighed my odds. *Triumph? Or disaster?*

She finished chewing. 'What do you want, Mother?'

What did I want? I wanted to bang her head on the counter! That's what I wanted.

I went with something more docile. 'I just want you to talk to me. I want to know what's going on in your world.'

She set her fork down and rested her fists on the counter on either side of the plate. 'Okay. Fire away.'

'It's not an interview, honey,' I said.

Why? Why? Why did I have to step on the landmine when I could see it? She had agreed to talk. It's all I wanted.

She looked down and mumbled, 'Then why does it feel that way?'

I was supposed to hear it of course. But I masterfully sidestepped that landmine. 'I just want to learn more about what you are doing. Your world, the world of technology—how it works with architecture. I don't understand much about it.'

Her body language relaxed and her eyes widened. She told me she was the assistant to the requirements manager of a new project and was helping the team with the technical specifications of the software.

'Requirements manager? Sounds important.' I was proud of her.

'Not the manager, Mother... The assistant...but yes, it is important.' She had somehow said all of that through another mouthful.

'I'm proud of you. I bet that will spruce up your college applications,' I commented.

But she was already back to reading.

I had to continue stoking. 'Are you planning to stick with the internship while you're at college?'

She hesitated. 'Um! Uh! Actually, that is something we should talk about.'

Hurrah! Now the lid is finally open. I said, 'Sure!'

'I've started hearing back from a few colleges...'

I couldn't imagine any college not wanting her on its roster. *Why is she hesitating?*

She continued, '...One of them is UCLA.'

'It's a good school,' I noted, too quick for my own benefit. She was just looking at me.

I got where she was going. *Put the lid back on! Put the lid back on! This is not the jar I wanted to open.*

I wish I hadn't reacted the way I did. 'Noooo... You're not thinking of moving, are you?' *It wasn't supposed to sound like a question.*

She already had the defence worked out. 'But you just said it's a good school. Even Sam...'

She broke off mid-sentence, which was better for my ego but the damage had already been done.

I imagined flailing my arms like a chimpanzee whose offspring was being taken away from her. I had to keep them caged—*both my arms and my offspring.* 'No! No! No! I thought we had talked about this, and you had decided to stay local.' I pointed my hands at her and started twiddling my fingers in an attempt to hypnotize her. 'UCLA is good...but NYU is better!'

She laughed, but sadly, it wasn't in agreement. 'I'm thinking UCLA will be better for me. I also want to continue studying Spanish.'

I knew this was about her. I hated that she had already

worked out a logical argument. I was desperate. 'But what about me?' I wish I hadn't.

She shot back, 'That's exactly the kind of emotional blackmail that I...'

That you what...that you what, Lily? I bit my lip. The warm texture of blood didn't go too well with the taste of the salad dressing.

'...want to avoid.' She had stopped eating too.

I changed tack. 'I'm sorry... I thought we had just started building on something...'

'Yes, Mother, but that has nothing to do with me going to college. Some independence will do me good.'

I had to ask. 'And are you saying you don't have independence here? You've got that and so much more... You've got the internship, a home, friends...'

She cut me off. 'That's not what I mean, Mother. There's nothing...'

Neither one of us got to the end of our sentences. I wasn't particularly excited about hearing the end of hers, but mine was going to be *...and you've got me.*

I felt a searing pain in my chest. It felt like a heart attack. *But I'm way too young and eat way too much salad for that.* I didn't know what to do.

I tried blackmail again. 'We've had such a rough journey and have just begun to mend our lives together. I was hoping to have at least three more years... There's so much more to share... I mean you still have your secrets... I'm afraid if we don't get a chance now, then we...'

And I broke down.

She slapped her hands down on the counter. 'Is that what this is really about—my secrets?'

135

'No! I just want you to trust me, Lily,' I said, shaking my head and sobbing.

'Oh! That's so unfair, Mom.'

She does like calling me Mom when I'm in pain.

'No, it's not! I only want what's best for you, but you can't exactly blame a mother for wanting the best...with you too.' I couldn't take it any more, and I started crawling up to my bedroom. I climbed slowly into bed and picked up my unfinished novel. I thought it might lift me up, but the words were just drippy blobs. Any chance that sleep might assuage my suffering was also thwarted by the sounds of her cleaning up downstairs. *If it isn't her music, it's something else.* I was fuming and thought I should have been stricter with her. *But how could I have been? She's already been through enough.*

◆

Revelation

It wasn't until much later that I heard a soft knocking on my door. 'Cynthia?' Lily was barely audible.

Oh! Back to Cynthia, is it? Isn't my pain deserving enough for 'Mom' now?

I barely got out a 'Yes dear.'

She came in and sat down on the corner of the bed. 'What're you reading?'

'Nothing,' I said, putting the book away. I had been holding it upside down anyway. 'That's not what's really on your mind now, is it?'

She smiled. 'No. I came to talk…to tell you…'

What else is left? After pulling the rug from under my feet…

She continued, '…that I trust you. There's something else too…I want to talk to you about. It's important.'

Is it the secret she had referred to over dinner with Sam? Not sure if I like the way he is becoming a part of our lives, I thought. My mind was in a shambles. I didn't know how much more I could handle that night.

I was still fixated on her leaving for another planet. 'More important than you leaving?' I wish I hadn't said it, but by then it was the Dark Lord of the Sith who was in control anyway!

It was her turn to avoid my sarcastic sashay. 'It's something different, Mother.'

Oh! Would you, for the love of god, stop calling me that!

'Is it about the letter? About Connor?' I asked, unable to contain myself.

'No.'

'Everything okay between you and Joanna?' I asked, concern filling my voice.

'Yes, Mother. Staawwp! I just want you to listen to me.'

It must be Roy, I thought. I hoped he wasn't back in her life. My concern had at least kick-started my heart again.

I kept quiet. She began slowly. 'You remember the night I broke up with Roy?'

First my heart, and now she wants to jolt my memory too? It had been some time back and he was not exactly a person I hoped to remember. I just nodded.

She must have seen through me. 'I had come back home crying and had gone straight to my room. It was pretty late, and you must have been worried because you came to check in on me…or at least you tried… But I had locked my door and said I didn't want to see you. Remember?'

Still, I was having trouble focusing my mind on the past. 'Mm…hmm…' I managed.

'You don't remember, do you?' she said, whacking her thigh with the back of her hand.

'Does it matter if I remember the night? What about that night, honey?' I asked as pleasantly as I could.

'It matters to me.' She slouched her shoulders. 'He did something bad that night.'

I knew he's a menace! I was still doing my best to keep quiet but was preparing for the worst.

'We had gone to CineStar—that drive-in theatre over by the casinos. They were having a special 'Halloween Screaming',' she said, rolling her eyes and making air quotes around 'Screaming'. 'There was Roy, Felicia, and her boyfriend David. There were a few others from school but they were in their own cars.'

She continued, 'Well…you should know I had no idea till that day…'

'What, dear?' I asked, in spite of myself.

She sighed. 'I didn't know it…but all three of them had been drinking. I think Roy had carried some with him and they had mixed it in their sodas. What was worse was…umm…they had been doing some drugs too. I swear I had no idea. I didn't even know what drug it was.'

It was the shock from hearing those words that kept me from squealing. I could taste the blood from my punctured lip oozing into my mouth again.

She went on. 'It was pretty late by the time I realized what was going on, and that theatre is, to be honest, in the back of beyond. I wanted us to call a cab or an Uber…'

I couldn't keep it in. 'As you should have!'

She looked up and her eyes were slivers. 'But he snatched my phone and wouldn't give it back. It was then, that instead of taking a cab, that jackass David suggested we go into Manhattan. He said his cousin was throwing a house party.'

She was stopping after every sentence. 'Even that bitch… didn't back me up. So I had a big fight with Roy and told him I was just going to sit there and not go anywhere… But it had gotten pretty late and the mall was closing down as well. So… they finally convinced me to get back into the car.'

I covered my open mouth with my hand to stifle a scream and mumbled, 'Nooo! You did not...'

She fidgeted but didn't get up. 'Mom! I really just need you to listen... I got back in on the condition that we would come back straight home.'

She paused. 'It was too late by the time I realized he was driving us to the city instead.'

I couldn't hold it in. 'Oh my god! He did not? I'm so glad he's out of your life, babe.'

'Mom!' She screamed. 'Will you just stop?'

I apologized.

She exhaled deeply before continuing, 'When I did realize, I screamed for him to stop right there and let me out. But he didn't. He just kept going faster and faster and then, just to piss me off, he switched off the lights and started waving his hands like a crazy person.'

'You should have just called the police,' I offered against my better judgement.

'Mother! This is exactly why...'

I was uncontrollably upset by then. 'If that boy did anything to hurt you... I'll kill him... I'll literally kill him!'

She stopped and got up from my bedside. 'Oh, really! Now you want to kill him? But that day in Mr Dean's office, you wouldn't even believe me. Unbelievable! I can't talk to you.'

She turned to leave. I had to control the situation. I had to control myself. 'I'm sorry! I'm extremely sorry! That's the last interruption, I swear. Why don't you just finish telling me what happened?'

'Nothing, Mother! Absolutely nothing happened. We stopped at the next gas station, but he still wouldn't give me my phone back. I tried using the phone there, when he was in the toilet, but he was out too quickly. That's when he snatched the receiver from my hand and hit me on the head with it. That's why we're not together any more. That's why I hit him when he was menacing me in school that day.'

She was glaring into my eyes. Her eyes were still mere slits. 'Happy? Now you know.' And she left.

All I had to be was quiet—what came naturally with my patients was not so easy with my own daughter. I was left with my memory of the many weeks when she had traded her spikes for a plethora of hats. She must have been trying to hide the bruise where Roy had hit her. As unbecoming as they had been, the hats had still been a welcome respite.

I was glad she was okay. *I would have killed him.*

◆

Tearing Down Walls

Sam had been busy at work, which was good for him. Challenges at work had been both distracting him as well as refuelling his 'mojo'. He had taken on Lily as his protégé, and that was working out well for her because she said she was learning a lot. He had his highs and lows but had been coping with the mood swings better. He had finally come to terms with the realization that moving forward was not tantamount to a betrayal of either his love for his family or of their memories.

What he had still not been doing, however, was talking about Marisa. We had found a safe slew of topics and I hadn't been able to shake them loose. Sam had been thwarting my consistent efforts to bring Marisa into our conversations. It had been more than a year since the tragedy and he hadn't even thought of starting to date. It was not his disinterest in dating that was a concern, but rather the possibility of him being in denial about the loss of his wife. I knew the more he prolonged such denial, the more debilitating it would be. I needed for him to confront his memories and the loss of his wife in order to ensure that he moved on and my job was done.

In one of my calls to check up on James, I asked him for his advice. He commented on how the truth of our confrontations matter immensely to our patients' well-being and suggested bringing up any such confrontation directly but sensitively. The choice of exploring any dimension must eventually be that of the patient so, before my next session with Sam, I had convinced myself the worst that could happen wasn't all that bad. If I was right then I would be able to help Sam address it and if I was wrong then he would tell me so.

◆

During the session, at what I thought was an opportune moment, I asked, 'How'd you meet Marisa?'

'What?' he asked, suddenly sitting upright and peering at me. 'Why is that relevant?'

I needed to be more direct. 'Just curious as to how you both met.'

That's a tautology! I was spinning my wheels. It was like some inexplicable and invisible force was tying me up.

'I really don't feel like talking about it,' he said, completely avoiding my gaze.

I rifled through my notes hoping that an answer or a strategy would miraculously present itself. My eyes fell upon a scribble about Marisa from one of our first few sessions. 'I remember you saying something about her never wanting to move back because her relationship with her family wasn't the best. Perhaps you want to tell me about that?'

He leaned forward and then teetered in the couch. I was afraid he was going to get up and leave, but he didn't. 'Where exactly are you going with this?' he gesticulated more fiercely than usual.

Where am I going? I wasn't sure. It seemed like I was going up against a wall, so I fought back. 'Sam, I've been trying to get you to talk about her for some time now, but you always move the conversation back to Will. Now, before you say anything, just hear me out…'

'No, I don't. What are you trying to insinuate—that I didn't love her or something?'

I needed to break through his defences. 'No, Sam. In fact, it's just the opposite. I understand you might be finding it very painful to dredge up her memories, but I think you've not really been confronting her loss. When you talk about how much you miss them, you really mostly talk about Will. Even the memories you recount…'

He interrupted me again. 'Enough! Enough!' He lowered his head to his hands and started massaging his temples. 'Why does it matter though? She's gone now.'

I gave it one last push. 'It matters, because I'm afraid that when you really start missing her, you won't be able to handle it.'

'But I won't!' he was shivering.

I was stunned. And then, my worst fear for an outcome of a session was realized—he looked up at me, apologized, said he 'couldn't go on', and left, much before our time was up.

I sat there paralysed, trying to reconstruct what had just happened. I had too many questions ricocheting in my head. I wasn't sure what he had meant by 'I won't'—did he mean he won't miss her or that he won't be able to handle it? I was also not sure about what 'couldn't go on' meant—did he mean he couldn't go on with our sessions or… I was petrified there was even another possibility. *What have I done? Have I brought the worst upon him…and myself?* I felt a shiver go up my spine.

◆

I had thought he had been doing so much better. I didn't know what to do so I texted him to check if he was okay. I waited for a reply, but didn't get one. Later in the evening when I was back home, I tried calling him but he didn't pick up. I even called 911, but disconnected before the call went through because I didn't know what I was going to say to them. *My patient is not picking up my calls and I'm having a psychological episode because of it,* was hardly 911-worthy.

The next day, I tried calling him again. I was sure he wouldn't pick up. In fact, when I heard the 'hello' from the other side, I thought it had gone straight to his voicemail and almost began to leave a message.

'Hello,' he said again.

That's when I realized it wasn't his voicemail. It was him! 'Hello Sam… Is that you?' *Who else could it be?*

'Yes. It's me.' No other explanation was forthcoming.

'Where are you? Are you okay?'

'Yes, Cynthia. I'm okay and I'm driving.'

'Driving…to where?' I didn't know where I was going with my question again.

'I don't know… Just driving.' He fell silent as if his response had been perfectly reasonable.

I tried to sound as calm as possible. 'What do you mean by just driving? I need to know if you're okay—I'm concerned about some of the things you said earlier, and…'

'Really, I'm okay. You needn't worry about me. I'm sorry I left in a rush but I just needed to get out of there and will let you know when I'm back.'

'And when might…' but he had already hung up. That's why I don't like cell phones—you can't even bang them down. Had it been a romantic relationship, I would have started preparing my I-think-we-should-start-seeing-other-people speech right about then.

Dam Bursts

After a couple of weeks, Sam finally called. He wanted to come in for a session at his usual time and wondered if I was still open. I thought about his choice of the word 'open' and silently went through a list of the choicest four-letter words of my own!

When he walked in for the session, he must have confused my stolid expression for bonhomie because he greeted me as if nothing had ever happened. I didn't say anything, so he finally broke the tension. 'I'm sorry. I realize what I did was very inconsiderate.'

I maintained an unruffled façade.

He continued looking at me. 'I know you have only my best interests at heart. It's just that you kept pushing me to talk about her and I really didn't want to.'

I wasn't sure what to do with that so I asked, 'And you're here now because you do?'

He continued staring at me. 'Not really...and not because I'm in some kind of denial, but...but because I think your concerns are unfounded.'

'And why is that?' I asked.

His shoulders slumped and he slowly leaned back into the couch. 'It's because…' He lowered his head and looked down before completing his sentence. '…I don't really miss her.' His eyes had welled up. His face was taut, red from the effort.

I didn't know what to make of it. Nothing in my training or experience had prepared me for an appropriate follow-up. For want of an apt response, I went with something equivocal. 'Do you feel like talking about that?' I should have just remained quiet.

He shot back, 'What's the point of asking that now? You haven't cared if I didn't, so far.'

That time, I did remain quiet.

He began slowly. 'Marisa and I… We didn't have the best of relationships. We really didn't have much left in fact…except for Will of course.' He paused briefly. 'I didn't want to live here. I had only moved here because I loved her, and she didn't ever want to move back. It was never even an issue for me, but our relationship was far from ideal and I really should have read the signs better. I had hoped she'd be able to change… She had been in therapy for a long time. She had already been divorced once because of her temperament and would promise to do better after each outburst. I still remember the day… It was before we were even married… It should have been the day I ended it but couldn't.'

I began to understand why he didn't talk about her. It was not because of denial but because he didn't want to dishonour her memory.

He took a few sips of water. 'She was heading out one morning… I held her really close and told her how much I loved her. She looked away at a plant we had bought together… A few of its leaves had just about started to wilt…and she said, "Oh my god! The plant—it's dying—it must be you." It took me years to realize... That's the day I should have left but couldn't... I was still in love with her. I guess I wanted to believe she could change.'

'Soon after... Will happened... So the decision was made for me. The alternative would have meant not having him in my life...and leaving him alone with someone I wasn't sure...' He didn't complete his thought.

A dam had suddenly burst. *And I had been thinking it was just a wall.*

When he spoke again, he sounded relieved. 'Can we please leave it at that? We don't need to talk more about this, do we?'

We needn't have. 'Sure,' is all I could rally. It may have been the only syllable I managed during his entire monologue. I may have even uttered it in response to a few other questions he asked but couldn't be sure about that either.

It struck me that he had made his peace with an untenable relationship with his wife because of Will. And had stuck around to protect him. *Something I hadn't been able to do for Lily.*

◆

I don't remember him leaving. Nor do I remember getting back home. As the rest of the day progressed, sure was the furthest from the way I felt.

A reminder prompted me about a date with Ryan. I wasn't sure if it was our second or third date. Although, when Ryan dropped me back that night, I had a sneaking suspicion there might not be a next one. I wasn't sure why I felt like that either—I had been perfectly pleasant all evening.

◆

I took Sam and his revelation to bed with me that night. I know the more our patients touch on our own unresolved issues, the more insecure and incompetent we feel about ourselves, but it was a strange, new sensation. Until then, I had thought he and I had been in the same boat, but rowing in opposite directions. That night, just before I drifted off, it dawned on me that perhaps we were both rowing in the same direction.

◆

Rebirth

For the next few days, Sam's revelation kept reverberating in my head. I wasn't sure why, but I felt I couldn't confront him. I was relieved that we didn't have a session scheduled for the next couple of weeks, but I was wrong.

It was the weekend and Lily woke up rather excited, reminding me of Sam's get together that evening. I had completely forgotten about it, but Lily was preparing for it with a gusto befitting her prom night. Between my love for her and my curiosity about not being able to get him out of my mind, I had little choice. I tried telling myself the sooner I met him and got it over with, the calmer I would be.

I was happier with the decision when I saw Lily emerge from her bedroom looking like the beautiful, young woman she was. She was wearing a pair of white pencil-pants with red polka dots, and a white poplin blouse with three-quarter sleeves and French cuffs. Her jacket, skinny belt and pumps were all accents of tan and complemented the getup very well. I gushed over her and wondered if I had seen the back of the punk phase permanently. She thanked me and her face turned the colour of the polka dots.

At least one part of my world is making some sense.

◆

Sam's place was a beautiful waterfront property in Westchester. By the time we made it, the party was in full swing. We might even have been the last ones to arrive. I was happy to see him socializing—the get together was a really good sign.

He greeted us effusively at the entrance. 'Welcome! Welcome to two of my favouritest people,' and proceeded to give us equally lavish hugs. I hadn't ever seen him in such high spirits and, as far as I could tell, it wasn't alcohol-induced either. He didn't complain about how late we were. I found myself complaining however, because I quickly realized the celebration was for his birthday and he had somehow managed to keep it a secret from both Lily and me. She didn't seem to care so much and was already mingling. She knew most of the people. It wasn't a very large group but was already kicking up a storm.

Even though it was his birthday, he looked like he had dropped a few years. He had lost some more weight and it was the first time I saw him clean-shaven. Buried under his beard had been a small but sharp scar—it ran from the bottom-corner of his cheek to just under his lip. He was dressed just as sharply. In a little less than a year and a half, I had mostly seen the sullen side of Sam. I was quite taken aback by that suave transition.

Then I noticed his home. It was a large house and the split-level layout accentuated its spaciousness. We entered the living room, which was a couple of steps lower than the dining and kitchen areas to the left. The entire space gave the impression of being outdoors because of the glass curtain-wall that ran the span of the front façade and afforded a view of the yard. It reminded me of James's perch overlooking Central Park. The yard itself was well maintained and I noticed a prominent bed of red and white flowers in bloom—the same ones he had brought for me and were William's favourite. *I still owe Lily their name*. I remembered Sam liked gardening and wondered if he did it all by himself.

The lighting was rich and there was a small fire flickering in a large wood-fireplace giving it a warm undertone. The infusion also accentuated the exposed-brick wall. At the far end of the living room, protruding from the wall, were broad, white steps—the staircase had a glass panel balustrade, making it look like it was suspended in air. The dining room had a slightly contrasting vignette. What had really caught my attention was the large island delineating the dining area from the kitchen at the back.

He offered me a glass of wine and proceeded to introduce me to his guests—mostly colleagues and their families. He was the perfect host, mingling deftly, looking into the arrangements, and making sure his guests were having a good time. Every so often he would check in on me as well. We were standing together and talking to a couple when, from the corner of my eye, I noticed a hand tap him on his shoulder, followed by a loud 'Happy Birthday, Uncle Sam!'

I almost lost my drink because that's what Lily called him, but the voice was definitely not hers.

Sam jumped too, and he smiled only after he had spun around. 'Major Matt!' he said in a friendly voice. 'Wait! You're not here to bust my party, are you?' They shook hands.

He was a tall and attractive man but he didn't look like a major. For one, he wasn't in the correct uniform. He laughed. 'No! But I could, if I get any complaints from the neighbours,' he winked at Sam.

It was Sam's turn to laugh. Major Matt continued, 'I'm still on duty, man, but I thought I'd quickly swing by and get some cake before it got over.'

'Ha! Ha! And I'm not going to stand in the way of a cop having his cake and eating it too!' While the major continued staring him down, Sam laughed even louder at his own silly joke. 'But don't you go harassing my guests! Speaking of which, let me introduce you around.' He looked around and realized we were alone—the couple we had been talking to had wandered off. 'That's just perfect!' he said, lowering his voice before continuing, 'You two are the most important people here anyway.'

'This is Cynthia. Remember, I told you about her—she's been so amazing. And her daughter's around here somewhere too.' He looked around, presumably for Lily.

'Of course! I've heard so much about you,' said the major, looking at me. 'Very nice to finally meet you.' He shook my hand, while I tried to make sense of it all.

Sam looked at me, 'You know him too, or rather you know of him. He's Sheriff Matthews—the other person who's been so helpful during the most difficult time of my life.'

'Oh! Then, in that case, I've heard about you too.' I laughed feebly hoping it would cover up my surprise. I felt a strong affinity towards him because I knew how helpful he had been to Sam during the investigation.

Sam turned to him, 'So are you saying you have to leave soon?'

'Sadly so,' he replied.

'Ah! That's a shame. Try…' but Sam couldn't finish his sentence.

'Sam! Sam!' Lily's high-pitched voice cut him off as she

153

REBIRTH

came hurtling towards him. She dragged him by the hand to attend to something that apparently couldn't wait, which left just the sheriff and me standing together.

'You're not a major, are you?' I asked, pointing at his uniform.

'Ha! What gave it away?' he replied. Apparently, he was just as cheeky.

I laughed. 'You're still on duty then, I take? Until when?'

'For another couple of hours, ma'am, but didn't want to be a no-show for his birthday.'

I felt agitated. *Even he knew it was Sam's birthday!* 'Oh! Please don't ma'am me,' I said sharply.

'Sorry! Just one of the perils of the job.'

'It's very nice of you to drop by,' I said, trying to make peace.

'No, really! Just came for the cake. He baked it himself.'

I laughed. 'No drinking then, I assume?'

He looked at me from under cocked eyebrows. 'You from Internal Affairs?'

I let out another laugh, 'I'm sorry... I don't know any cops.'

'Ha! Ha! No worries. Not for a couple of hours at least— maybe I'll have to come back for a nightcap!' He paused briefly, 'That's your daughter, Lily? The one who took him?'

I was shocked. 'Yeah, but how'd you know?'

His response was quick. 'I don't know if you've noticed... This one's a talker...surely you already must know that?'

We both laughed.

Sam came back with cake. 'Stop conspiring! Don't you have some police work to do? Here you go,' he said, offering the cake to the sheriff.

The sheriff contorted his face. 'What's this?'

'Cake,' Sam said. 'You wanted some, right?'

'Yeah I did, but this is just a crumb,' he said, wolfing it

down in a jiffy.

Sam and I laughed.

'There's more where it came from,' Sam said as he took my hand. 'Now come on, mingle already.'

The sheriff stayed put. 'No, really, I do have to go. I just came to wish you, and as you can see, my work here is done,' he said, handing the empty plate back to Sam.

Sam continued holding my hand. 'Like I was saying, that's a shame indeed. Try and swing by later—I have a Cuban with your name on it.'

I didn't know Sam smoked cigars.

The sheriff's eyes lit up. 'Enticing! I'll let you know if I can.'

'Well then, officer... Don't mind if I be stealing this treasure from under your nose,' Sam said, pulling me back into the party. 'Be seeing you.'

The sheriff laughed. 'It's not like I can run after you, you know.' He threw a pleasantry back at us. It got muffled by my heart, which was racing in response to Sam's cheesy flirtation.

I was happy that not only was Sam socializing again, but also making new friends. *Perhaps there is rebirth in some strange way after all.*

◆

Parrying

The party went off fabulously. The people were friendly and the food was great. The cake was definitely the highlight—he had indeed baked it himself. It wasn't very late though by the time I realized that most people had either left or were about to. Lily was clearly having a great time and could easily have been confused as the hostess—she was standing beside Sam and saying goodbye to most people. We were literally the last ones left and were about to take our leave when something inexplicable came over me. 'We'll stay and help you clean up a bit. It's the least we can do—for not bringing you a gift.'

Lily shot a look at me. 'Wha…?' And then turned to Sam. 'Have you seen my mother? She was just here.'

He laughed and said, 'I guess it's fair—the last to come in and the last to leave—but only on one condition. You don't help clean up,' he said, pointing at the catering crew that had already begun the onerous chore.

'Oh, right!' I said, noticing them for the first time. *How had I missed them?*

He led us to the kitchen. 'Coffee?'

'Tea please,' Lily and I said over each other.

I felt at home. We chatted as he brewed the beverages. Lily was still supercharged, sharing 'gossip with the boss', according to her.

I told Sam, 'I think it'll be decaf for her, please.' He laughed.

Lily opened her mouth slightly and let her head and her eyes roll back. She sidestepped the comment and asked me, 'What did you think of the cake? He baked it.'

She knows about Sam as much as I do! 'It was great—couldn't get enough!'

He said something about how he got into baking and what he liked about it. 'It was the precision, not to mention the sugar! But this one—this one had a deep, dark, secret ingredient. Can you guess what?'

'What?' I echoed.

'Let me explain how this very complex game of guessing works,' he said, looking straight at me.

'Oh, sarcasm, eh?' I almost reached over and whacked him. 'Fine… Cinnamon.'

'Yeah sure, but that's not really that much of a secret.'

'Ginger,' I tried again.

He paused, tilted his head, and then applauded patronizingly. 'Give the contestant a cigar! What gave it away? Was it the gingerbread?'

'I'm going to whack you,' I said, punching his shoulder gently.

His eyes lit up. 'Whiskey!'

He was first to notice Lily. She was not into the guessing game but was staring deep into her tea. 'You okay there, Lily?'

'Yaaaa,' she said, not sounding sure at all. 'I was just thinking about the secret.'

157

'You mean the whiskey? I wouldn't worry about it—it was less than an ounce—see, your mom couldn't even...'

'No! I mean just the secret.'

Sam and I looked at each other. I wondered if he was thinking the same thing I was.

She continued, 'You remember? That night, when you were at our place, you said something about secrets and how it's good to talk about them?'

'Yes.' He stole another glance at me. I wondered if he recalled the conversation.

'What happens when you can't?' she asked.

'You mean you can't talk about them?'

'Mm...hmm,' she said.

'Umm... is this secret hurting you in any way?' Sam probed.

'Not really,' she said.

'Not really, or not at all?' he asked, straightening up.

It's a good question, I thought.

She bit her lip. 'Umm... It only hurts my conscience.'

Wait a minute—she has already told me her secret—is there more? And why is it hurting her conscience?

'Hmm...that does sound like a bit of a bind. Trust me, I know the feeling,' he said scratching his clean-shaven chin. 'Then it's better to try and share it with someone you trust it will be safe with, and see how your conscience feels after.'

'What do you mean by "safe with"?'

Is this a different secret she is talking about? Is this about Connor? About us?

'That they won't tell anyone.' He paused before adding, 'Or that won't hurt them.'

'But...what if they don't understand...or don't listen?' She was looking at Sam, but I realized she was talking about me. *It is…about us.* My insecurity from not knowing another secret was rapidly replaced by an insecurity about my little gerbil ratting me out! It was my turn to dunk my face in my cup of tea.

He stopped scratching his chin. 'Well, you can't hope everyone will be the way you would like them to be. And really, it's about your conscience, so what matters most is that your secret is safe.'

She was silent for a while. He looked at me and raised his eyebrows. It could have either meant 'any idea what this is about?' or 'how am I doing here?' The only thing I cared about was keeping my poker face on.

It was Lily who finally broke the silence. 'But wouldn't it be better if they listened?'

He was clearly up to the task. 'See—sometimes—when I would tell my parents stuff, they would get all huffy and would try to take matters into their own hands, but I knew they wouldn't tell on me. That was most important. When I grew up, I still needed to talk to them and, by then, I could also tell them what I expected or needed from them. They would still get hassled and throw a fit, but then they would apologize and everything would go back to being okay. All I needed to know for sure was that they had my back.'

'Hmm…' she trailed off.

'And you know—your mother—she is like the best secret-ary ever!' He said 'secret-ary' with air quotes and accompanied his silly wordplay with a wink in my direction.

I was sipping on my ice-cold tea, and it erupted through my nose. They both laughed. I wasn't amused.

Lily's expression finally softened. 'I know you keep saying that, so what about you?'

'What about me, what?' His brows jumped up.

She shrugged. 'You know—your secrets? Have you shared them with her?'

He got up from the bar stool. 'What secrets? What'chu talkin' 'bout Willis?' I laughed because I knew he was parrying by using a popular catchphrase from a late-'70s sitcom. Obviously, it didn't work on Lily because there was no way she would have even heard about the show. 'Know thy audience, Sam!' I blurted out.

Lily didn't give up. 'Oh c'mon now! I'm not a child.'

Sam looked around the kitchen. 'Really...she knows everything... Care for some more tea? No? Okay!' He started pouring tea into his cup; only he had been drinking coffee!

I stared at him. Lily cracked up. 'Fine! It's none of my business anyway.'

I just hoped the incriminating conversation was finally over. Lily didn't agree with me though. 'What if it's not enough?'

He drained his cup in the sink. 'What do you mean?'

She explained, 'I mean just sharing it with someone...is not enough...and my conscience needs more?'

He looked back at her. 'That depends on what it is. When you share it with your secret-keeper, you might get better advice about what to do. I have realized, that unless some harm can come from it, confronting secrets always helps. Perhaps I have some work to do there myself... But then, who doesn't?'

I wondered if she had been thinking about confronting Roy, or Connor perhaps, but my thoughts remained half-baked. I didn't see it coming, and apparently neither did he.

She looked up at him, left her seat, and hugged him.

'Oof!' He was taken by surprise but still hugged her back. 'It's okay, Lily—everything will work itself out.'

He looked at his watch. 'You know it's getting rather late. Why don't you both stay over? The guest room is always ready.'

I could handle being impressed with suave Sam but sleeping over at Sam's was a line I didn't want to cross. I declined politely and thanked him for his offer as well as his gracious hospitality. He walked us to our car.

◆

Once on our way, I asked Lily, 'Did you have a good time?'

'Oh yeah! The best,' she said, and continued looking at me.

I have to do better at listening to her. The rest of the drive back home, we both stayed silent.

◆

Pulling on a Thread

My phone beeped a few minutes after we got home. It was a text from Sam. 'Thanks for making it and for the great birthday gift! Hope you're both tucked in safe and sound.'

I replied. 'Ha! Ha! Yes we are, and it was a super evening.'

Another beep. 'I'm sorry if I said too much to her.'

I replied. 'No. Don't be silly. I think you were great. Any better and I might be out of a job.' I added a winking emoji.

He responded, 'LOL! I don't think so.'

I kept looking at the text window. I saw the ellipsis moving in waves, but soon it stopped. I felt a different kind of a wave—it was a small one, but of disappointment. I wasn't sure why. I had met him and was calmer after all. But at first, I couldn't fall asleep—I just kept tossing and turning. Then a few minutes later, my phone beeped again. 'By the way, you were looking very nice. Red and white suits you…both! Sleep tight!'

And I did.

◆

The day after, Sam called unexpectedly. I picked up the phone with a smile. We exchanged a few pleasantries. I was sure he hadn't called for that but I went along.

A couple of minutes in, he said, 'Umm…the reason I'm calling is…well…let me ask you this… How do you think we're doing?'

'What do you mean?' I really wasn't sure what he meant.

'I've been thinking that recently I've been doing much better. It's mostly thanks to you and…'

I gasped, 'Oh my god, Sam! Are you breaking up with me?'

'Ha…ah… huhk…huhk!' I think he meant to laugh, but all I heard was weird choking sounds.

'Are you okay?' I asked, a little concerned.

He took his time. 'Not really. I wasn't expecting that. I guess I'm not…but rather I'm suggesting we should stop seeing each other…at work. Your work that is.'

It was my turn to choke. I felt the need to end that back and forth, even though I didn't want to.

He continued, 'But I'm also not saying we should start seeing other people.' He had recovered well.

I should have expected no less, I thought. 'I think you are right—you have been doing much better, and it's totally your call. Besides, you know exactly where to find me!'

Before we hung up, we decided on a wrap-up session a week or so from then. After we disconnected, I felt happy for him. He was finally moving on with his life. I was a little disappointed too that I wouldn't be seeing him as often. I looked back at my notes and was reminded of his revelation from our previous session. I closed my notebook and slowly ran my fingertips over the colourful tiles of the dragon. My doubts about why I had struggled to pull at that thread of his life came coasting back in. They floated around in the back of my mind for the rest of the day and I took them to bed with me at night.

In bed, my doubts decanted into my dreams. I dreamt about our sessions. And about him.

I woke up with a start. My dreams led me to a discovery. I had pussyfooted around the topic of his wife—not for fear of exposure of my own insecurities, but rather of the way I had begun to feel. When I had pulled on that thread from his life, I hadn't realized I'd be pulling on one from my life too. And given that I had, the fabric of my emotional defence all but unravelled.

And then my discovery was devoured by disbelief. I had fallen for him!

It just isn't possible! I have spent years carefully quarantining myself from such emotions and had a set of stringent strategies including, but not restricted to, reminding myself of my marriage…

That's where my thoughts trailed off because I realized the chink in my armour. Ever since the demise of my marriage, I hadn't had that recourse.

Has that been my undoing? Have I survived a decade-long career without a single case of transference, only to trip up now, like this, by letting myself become the object of it?

Oh, no! No! No! I hadn't even been attracted to him, or had I? Oh please, make it stop! I pinched myself and winced in pain. It was all too much for 4 a.m. *I need coffee.*

I didn't know if I was more upset that I had let myself feel that way or that I couldn't do anything about the way I felt. That it was a conundrum, made it even worse. After all, such feelings should be uplifting, and it had been a very long time since I had felt anything even vaguely similar. As the caffeine started to clear some of the slush, I remembered he had broken up with me, at work, which provided only a modicum of respite.

◆

I spent the next few days diligently reminding myself of all the years of training, including that on ethics, and crossing off all my strategies. By the end of the exercise, I had been able to convince myself to hoard my feelings. I had even decided I didn't need to discuss it with James. *I am a professional after all.*

Besides, I realized that during this internal imbroglio I hadn't really thought of him—I mean, all I was doing was think of him but I hadn't thought of how he might feel. In all likelihood, he just thought of us as friends…if that.

◆

Courage

Given the state of my relationship with Lily for most of the previous year, it was usually my work that kept me sane. It was a tumultuous twist that it had become the other way round. Still, I needed to have an intervention with her—more for myself than for her. Focusing on that had kept me from unravelling completely. I kept rehearsing what I would say but could not get it right. One evening, as we were finishing dinner, I took the plunge. 'Babe, could we talk for a bit, please?'

'Mm…hmm, I am listening,' she said, while burying her nose perceptibly deeper into her magazine.

'No, I really need you to listen to me this time,' I insisted.

She closed the magazine and looked up. I could see she had discreetly stuck in her finger on the page she had been on.

It was going to have to be enough, so I started. 'I know it may seem that I don't listen to you or that I don't understand you, but it's not because I haven't been trying. I think it's because I've been putting a lot of pressure on myself.'

'Okay, Mother. Thanks!' She started flipping open the magazine again.

I had more to say. 'Ahem! I also want to say that I'm sorry. I'll try to be more patient from now on. I just want you to know you can trust me.'

'Gotcha!' She shot at me with her index finger, and started to get up to leave.

She's just testing me, I thought. *I must do more. I have to make her believe me.*

I went off script and regretted it immediately. 'If going to UCLA is what will make you happy then that's what you should do.' A shiver shot up my spine, but for her it worked like magic.

'Really?' she gushed. 'You mean it? Oh Cyn...Mom! That means the world to me.' She rushed to give me a hug. 'Thank you. You're the best!'

'Aren't I?' I said happily. *I'm screwed,* I thought sadly.

There was a spring in her step. She even offered to clean up. I didn't want to rain on her parade, especially with my tears, so I excused myself and started the arduous ascent to my bedroom.

◆

I was barely halfway up the stairs when I heard her say, 'Mom,' ever so softly.

I leaned against the banister.

She was facing me but looking down at the floor. 'There's something I need to talk to you about as well.'

What is it now? It's too soon for another test.

'Sure, love.' I sat down, right there on the stairs.

She walked to the stairway and plonked herself on the bottom step. 'That night...when Roy hit me...something else happened too.'

I bit my tongue. After all, I had just promised her that I'd listen better.

She straightened her back against the wall as if she was bracing herself. 'When he switched off the lights and was waving his hands...and I screamed at him...he didn't stop the car... But something did...'

Did they have an accident? But she's okay. I mentally went through a checklist of her friends who were with her that night and tried recollecting the last time I had seen them—they had all been hearty.

'...Or rather, almost did. It was too late by the time we saw it—there was a deer just standing there in the middle of the road.'

She didn't look at me even once while she spoke. 'We would have seen it had our lights been on. It saw us literally at the last second and jumped onto the other side of the highway. Luckily for us, I had put my hands on the wheel. I swerved, Roy slammed on the brakes, and we skidded to a stop.'

Phew!

'That's when it happened, Mom.' She started crying.

What? What happened? Didn't she just say they had stopped?

I put a hand on her shoulder. 'It's okay, honey. Take your time.'

She shuddered as she started speaking again. 'We heard a loud crash from behind us. It was on the other side of the road. We looked over and, even though we couldn't see the deer, we saw the lights of a car. It had swerved off the road and...' She finally looked up at me teary-eyed. '...and it had crashed Mom... Its horn was stuck and we could hear that too.'

She was sobbing uncontrollably by then. 'And...and Roy just took off, Mom. I tried stopping him so we could go back, but he just kept going. There was no one else there at the time.

We might have been able to do something to help, but he just kept going. He said something about the drinks and the drugs… David and Felicia were freaking out too.'

I felt like I was falling through a void. *Why is it I keep falling on these stairs?* I was grasping the edge of the tread for dear life.

On the one hand I was relieved that Lily and her friends were okay, but on the other hand, I was panicking, thinking that it sounded way too familiar for my liking.

How do I find out?

My head was buzzing. It was unbearable. I tried to remember where Marisa and Will's accident had happened but I couldn't. I also didn't want to ask Lily any questions because she needed me to be present for her.

She was speaking through clenched teeth. 'He just kept driving, Mom. He didn't stop, no matter how much I screamed. I wanted to call the police to let them know, but he still had my phone. We stopped at the next gas station, but that was because Felicia needed to pee. I found a phone at the back and tried to call the police—that's when he snatched the receiver from my hand and hit me. We might have been able to help, Mom…' A fresh wave of sobs overwhelmed her.

I shimmied down and took her into my arms. 'It's okay, my love. It's over now.'

Things were anything but okay in my world. I fought very hard to stay focused but my grip was weakening. I could do little but be there for her in silence. It seemed like hours before I finally tucked her in.

It will be a lifetime before I sleep next.

◆

Post-truth

My thoughts kept me up all night. *Could they have caused Marisa and William's accident? What are the chances? There was clearly no report of an animal but that doesn't say much.*

Was she the 'passer-by' who had called the police? Sam had said something about a public telephone, but not a gas station.

When was this? I need to get the dates, the location. I need more information. I need to get to the bottom of this. But I was already at the bottom...of an abyss.

All of a sudden, I was the one with more secrets than I could handle. I had been able to put away my feelings for Sam for the past few days, but they all came flooding back.

◆

The next morning, we had our cereal in silence. I had little more to offer her except solace.

She needed more. 'What do you think I should do?'

Ironically, it was something Sam had said at his place that came to my rescue. 'You remember what Sam said the other day...about confronting...'

She cut in. 'You mean I should go to the police?'

I haven't thought it through. 'Or…' I offered, hoping there would be another interruption. None was forthcoming, so I had to improvise. 'Perhaps talk to Roy?'

'No way! He hit me, Mother. I can't stand for that. I don't want to be like…'

I was thankful she didn't get to the end of her sentence. I had to tell myself to stay focused. 'What do you think I meant when I said you should talk to Roy?'

'Er… I should tell him how I feel.'

I had at least exposed a doubt. 'Kind of… I meant you should confront him and ask him to go to the police. After all…'

'Oh! That way…hmm… Let me think about it.'

'You should. Either way, I'm glad you spoke to me. I know it took a lot of courage.' I hugged her tightly. 'I can't imagine what this must have been doing to you.'

Now she can't imagine what this is doing to me, and what it would do to Sam. 'No matter what you decide, let me know if you need me…in any way.'

'Sure! Thanks, Mom,' she said.

I knew it was getting late but I had a few questions of my own I really needed to ask her too. *Now is as good a time as any.* 'Where did you say this happened, babe?'

'I told you, Mom—I don't really remember. I didn't realize he was driving us into the city till much later. I do remember the gas station though…hmmm…' she trailed off.

Okay, that didn't help. I had one last shard of hope. 'And when was this again?'

'I knew it! I knew you didn't remember the night we broke up…humph… This is why I was upset the other night too you know…because it was the night before my last birthday.'

All of a sudden, I wished I hadn't asked that question. Now there was no room for doubt...or rather hope that it wasn't them that had caused the accident. I looked at her nonplussed.

She left for work without having had a bite of her cereal. My own bowl of Froot Loops—those tiny, colourful lifebuoys—had become mush.

◆

What do I do now? I need another plan, for a different problem. There is no light at the end of the tunnel.

I needed to see James. Instead, I went to the movies. I love movies and I hadn't seen one in a while. I couldn't think of a better time to escape. So I watched two, back to back.

◆

I was still trying, in vain, to make sense of my world when I walked back into the house later that afternoon. I heard sobbing from the kitchen. *It has to be Lily. What is she doing at home? Shouldn't she be at work? Why is she crying?*

'Lily?'

I heard a feeble 'Yes.'

I hurried towards the kitchen and saw her doubled up. I caressed her head. 'What happened, darling? Are you okay?'

'Yes...I mean...no,' she said. 'I went and met Roy.'

And what did the menace do now? I swear I will... I stopped my thoughts from running amok. All I said was, 'And?'

She shuffled but didn't look up. 'I spoke to him, what else? I told him what we did was wrong and that we should go to the police. He told me to lead by example.'

'What does that mean?' I couldn't help myself.

She looked up at me through bloodshot eyes. 'He said I should apologize to him first for the incident at school and thank him for not pressing charges. Apparently that's what he was trying to do that day. He had one helluva way to force his apology on me! He's such a bully!'

That I know.

She continued, 'I tried controlling myself, Mom, but I couldn't. And we ended up fighting.'

My concern got the better of me. 'Are you okay? Did he harm you? Is that why you're crying?'

She looked at me incredulously. 'No! I'm crying because of you, Ma... I mean us.'

The only sound that escaped my mouth was 'Oh!' *Is this because of my suggestion to go and confront him?*

She looked away. 'Well, he's been sober for months now and has even been going for counselling.'

And what does that have to do with me?

She had stopped crying by then. 'It made me realize something about us...and I want to say I'm sorry...'

Sorry? 'Sorry for what, my dear?'

'Sorry for being such an ass to you, Mom... I should have at least given you and us a chance.'

Nothing. I was not getting any of it. *My world is topsy-turvy enough as it is.*

She sighed. 'I should have taken ownership, Mom—for my situation. When I should have come and spoken to you and told you what he was doing to me, all I did was blame you.'

She is talking about Connor, and not Roy!

She continued. 'I blame myself for not having had the strength to share it with you... I should have, Mom... I should have.'

I took her in my arms. 'Oh, my darlin'! You have nothing to blame yourself for. We were in it together and, besides, it's all over now. It's okay, Lily.'

'I love you Mom…so much.'

'I love you too, babe,' I said, hugging her even tighter.

It was the first time in years she was calling me 'Mom' without seeing me in pain. *She doesn't know.*

'I'm so glad Sam put whiskey in that cake.' She tried laughing in between sobs, but had little success.

It took a minute for the penny to drop. And then, I knew what I had to do. I was going to be as courageous as Lily, and untangle the mess.

◆

Walking the Plank

It took me a day or so to acknowledge that courage by itself wasn't going to cut it—it was just one of the ingredients. The other ingredient, one I still needed, was a strategy. I had to figure out whom to drop the bombshell on first, and how. On the one hand, I couldn't reveal details about Sam to Lily, and on the other hand, I didn't want to reveal this to him without checking with her first. That's where I hoped James would be able to help.

◆

I surprised myself by being able to enjoy the walk from the station to James's place. It was already warm out and it was a nice day. It felt strange to be walking the plank, on such a beautiful day. I decided to savour the feeling and took the longer detour, which ended up being through the Transit Museum, a place whose delights I found very restorative.

As I was about to step in, I saw a poster for a special gallery talk on the history of the Grand Central. I immediately perked up and felt good about having taken the detour. I was further buoyed when I saw that it was on a special day—my birthday. *It'll make a befitting birthday present to myself.*

I wished I had someone to go to the talk with and I found myself thinking of Sam. I whooshed the thought away—I couldn't afford to be distracted from my dilemma. More importantly, there was no way I could let James find out about my feelings. They weren't relevant—to James.

I still had some time and I walked over to the kiosk to buy a solitary ticket. My excitement didn't last long—the event was sold out.

The disappointment blotted out the museum's restorative power and I found myself back, fighting demons, on the street. I sought solace in the fact that both Sam and Lily had been able to vanquish their demons and find peace. *For the time being at least.*

Before I knew it, I was at James's. I was afraid of walking in and girded myself before ringing the doorbell. He opened the door and flashed a smile that would ordinarily set a thousand ships to sail. *But not this one, and not on this day.*

He looked at me and flinched. 'Whoa! What's with the aura, young lady? Looks like you need this cane more than I do.' He waved his cane mischievously, quite possibly in an attempt to cheer me up. It didn't work.

He got the hint. 'Okay. Not that kind of house call. Everything all right? Lily okay?'

'Meh! I'm not gonna lie to you, James—things could be better, much better.' I wanted to both laugh and cry at my situation. 'It's kind of everything and everyone.'

'Oh boy! This does sound dire,' he said, moving the cookies aside and setting his pipe down on the table.

I didn't know where to begin. I tried explaining my dilemma

without violating Sam's confidentiality and finished with, 'I do feel there might be this teeny, tiny chance their stories are not about the same incident, but I think that's just wishful thinking.' That it was wishful thinking was, quite literally, the only part I felt confident about.

I took a deep breath. 'I think the real question in front of me is who I should talk to first—Lily or the patient?'

It was his turn to stare sombrely at me. 'Well, it doesn't matter if they are the same incident or not.'

'What do you mean?'

'If they aren't, then there's nothing to worry about. And if they are, you still have to get this off your chest.' He made sense. *No surprises there.*

'However,' he continued, 'more importantly...'

There is something more important than this?

'...how is the patient doing?'

'He's been doing much better, in general and at work. Oh! Did I forget to mention? Lily's doing an internship with him.'

'Oh!' He began stroking his beard.

I continued, 'At first he was struggling to move past anger, but then he slowly started reconciling with his loss after I got him to open up about his family like you had suggested. And he's been healing steadily ever since. But he still wouldn't talk about his wife, and I thought it was because he was in denial. Only much later did he confess that they didn't have the best of relationships—she had some anger and abuse issues, and...'

'Mm...hmm...' He stopped stroking his beard.

Even though I hadn't been paying attention to his responses, the intonation of that one got the better of me. 'What? What does that mean?'

'Nothing,' he said.

I wasn't buying it. 'What do you mean, nothing? Say it or you'll choke on that smile, and I really don't have time for that today.'

He laughed. 'So then, here's the most important question—how are your feelings towards your patient?'

Wait... What? Why would he ask that? How could he have known? I revolted inside. Somehow, I managed a 'What do you mean?'

He called me right out. 'Don't be evasive, young lady. Don't forget whom you are talking to, and that you came here for help. Hiding stuff isn't going to help either one of us. Neither one of us knows how much time I have left. If you hide stuff now, you might never...'

I had to cut him off. 'Okay, okay! Stop. You can't use that for everything.' I fidgeted. First, I pleaded guilty. 'Actually, I'm not sure. Of late, I've been aware... I may have started...developing feelings for him. I don't know how it's possible.' Then I offered my defence. 'In the past, reminding myself of my marriage and my family is all I needed to do to keep any kind of emotion in check, but now... I just didn't see it coming, James.'

His voice was as soft and comforting as ever. 'It's only natural, Cynthia. You are a loving, caring, and genuine person and that's gone unrequited for quite some time. And then this person comes into your life—who's the object of your care, builds a strong rapport with Lily, and has an abusive ex-partner in common...' He knew he needn't say more, so he followed up with: 'Any idea since when you might have been feeling like this?'

'None,' I said, avoiding his stare. I'm sure he knew but he didn't let my blatant evasion bother him.

He moved on with the matter at hand. 'I do see your quandary. The way I see it, you can go both ways with this.'

My mind did a somersault in delight. *I have some choice in the matter!*

'You could tell your patient first and then ask him not to confront Lily till you have had the chance to clear things up with her. Or you could tell Lily first and ask her how she might want to handle it, although that might be a bit much for her. Either way, you needn't ask their permission to tell the other one, just manage their expectations.'

Easier said than done. We talked a little more about pros and cons till I felt I had what I needed. On my way out, I had to ask, 'You didn't ask me what I was going to do about my feelings?'

'Because I don't need to,' he replied. 'Darling, I know you better than you think I do.'

Perhaps even better than I know myself. I'm not about to let him in on that secret though. 'Thanks, James! That means so much to me. I love you.' I gave him a tight hug. As I moved away, I noticed a moist patch on his light-blue linen shirt. I hadn't realized I'd been crying. 'Sorry that I'm running out on you like this today, but I'll come again real soon.'

'Take your time, love… I'm not going anywhere.' He winked.

◆

On the train ride back home, as the concrete of the city gave way to the green of the trees and the blue of the sky, I began thinking more clearly. I was going to share the truth with Sam first, and then with Lily. I felt better, although I wasn't sure I could afford to.

◆

Backflip

I had been bolstering my resolve for the moment when Sam would walk in through the door. I was trying to maintain momentum and brace for impact at the same time—as if I was about to take off knowing I was destined to crash-land. It was his last, wrap-up session and I had to come clean, but I still hadn't exactly worked out how.

When he walked in, my heart fluttered but I wasn't ready for how serious he looked. I wondered if he could make out my state of mind.

I assumed his stress had to do with work and that it wouldn't come in the way of my revelation. *Then it will all be over. Or will it just be the beginning?*

For the first time, he fell into the leather armchair instead of the couch—*how befitting that he should be embracing change.*

'Everything okay?' I asked. 'You seem pensive.'

'It's because I am,' he said, crossing his legs. His body language belied his response and he sounded surprisingly calm. 'And as to whether I'm okay, I'm not sure. Apparently, someone came forward and shared details of the accident.'

Oh my god! Roy went to the police. Oh my god! Sam knows.
I wished for a giant sinkhole to open up right there and then.
I whispered, 'When?'

Sam stared at me, forcing me to look away, then said, 'Why
does that matter?'

It didn't. I turned my gaze back towards him. It took a
colossal effort to look into his eyes—I was hiding way too much.
I prayed the look in his eyes was because of the interruption
and nothing else. Come to think of it, it took a colossal effort
to even continue breathing—my conscience was choking me. I
realized I had been steadily scraping away at the dragon's tiles
on my notebook.

'A young boy named Rob...or Ron...or something like
that,' he paused.

It's Roy! But I was too afraid to correct him, for fear of
finding out the truth and losing the last beacon of hope that his
family's accident was a whole different saga from Lily's incident.
I was still grasping at straws.

'He saw it happen.' Sam continued looking at me, and I
had to look away again.

I knew it was really not about me—it was about him. I
had to assess if he was showing any signs of regression. *How
much does he really know?*

He continued drumming the armrest with his fingers. 'Aren't
you curious?'

Not really, I thought. 'Yes I am, but I want you to take
your own time.'

'It was a deer! The boy said it first jumped in front of him
and then over to the other side. He saw the car swerving...'

Words stumbled out of my mouth. 'Did they check?'

'What?' He stopped dead. 'Wait!' He uncrossed his legs

181

slowly and leaned forward. He waited for some time before starting again. 'I'm telling you—he saw it in his rear-view mirror and then the car vanished. He thought it had managed to avoid...'

I jumped in again. 'Did they call it in?'

He smiled.

Why is he smiling? How insensitive! Oh wait! That would be me.

'Now you're curious. You can't even let me finish. And... it's just the boy who went to the police.'

Oh shit! I was surprised Roy had gone to the police but I wasn't surprised his confession had some embellishments and omissions. Meanwhile, on my notebook, Gaudí's embellishment was all but scraped away. I was alone.

'That's the thing,' he said, raising a finger. 'He said he tried calling but didn't have good network coverage and the call kept getting disconnected. But something doesn't add up—the 911 call had been from a landline at some gas station.'

The room was getting smaller and hotter by the second. 'Maybe it's because there were more than one...'

He got up, not letting me finish. 'Exactly! You and I—like one mind. That's what I thought, but the report clearly mentions just the one call. And that too, from a woman.'

Had he let me finish, I would have said, 'More than one person in the car.' It was meant to be the opening of my confession.

The buzzing in my head was driving me insane. I couldn't say anything then—he was still standing—I needed him to be seated. It would help—*especially if I needed to make a hasty escape.*

He did finally sit down on the couch, closer to me. 'Let's just say I was willing to believe his story. What I really don't understand is this—if he didn't see the accident and if he didn't cause it, then why go to the police at all?'

Who is he...all of a sudden now? Sherlock Holmes?

He continued, 'I asked Matthews if he'd let me talk to the boy—I'd like to run him under cold water just for a bit—but apparently it's against policy. Humph! Policy-shmolicy! Instead, he suggested "I drop it". I wanted to drop him...and...I want to drop in on the boy...'

He jumped back up and started pacing. What was strange, however, was that even though he was pacing, he was still composed. None of the anger from the past resurfaced. I thought we had done some good work together and, even in that dreary moment, I felt a pang of pride.

He looked at his watch but continued to pace. 'Or at least... it's what I thought I wanted...at first.'

Time was running out and I was sure my next patient was already waiting outside. I had to interrupt him. 'Why don't you sit down and let's talk about it? In fact, I have something to tell you as well,' I offered in a renewed attempt.

He kept standing and looking down at me. 'You already did—you are the one who told me to get some answers, right? That's what I thought I needed too, but...'

I could put an end to his misery, and mine as well. I wanted to scream to make him listen to me but I wasn't able to muster the strength. I hadn't expected Roy to have gone to the police. *Why hadn't Lily told me? Maybe she doesn't know either.* I hadn't expected Sam to know and then be so calm about it. I hadn't imagined I'd be feeling the way I did about him.

I gave it one last push and didn't let him finish. 'But I can help with that.'

'You've already helped so much,' he continued. 'You know, I've been afraid I'm doing something crazy. You've pulled me back from the brink and you've been so patient.' He looked at his watch again. 'I know we're out of time but I think you may have been right. I think I'd like to come in for one final session. I'd like to get more out of my system—especially how I've been handling this new information.'

Final…sounds foreboding. Tell him… Tell him now!

He may have said something about deciding on a date for the final session, but I couldn't be sure. A voice was screaming inside my head and it was drowning out all other sounds. My head was in a tizzy. I thought I was going to pass out.

'Cynthia!' His hand was on my shoulder. It brought me back.

We agreed to meet the next day itself.

Perfect! I can't think of anything else I'd much rather be doing. The thought of the gallery talk at the Transit Museum flashed, albeit briefly. *Just as well I couldn't get the tickets.*

I don't remember when he left. But when he did, it was clear my plan had been foiled. I thought it had been foolproof. It had to change—I had to tell Lily first. Perhaps that would give me the strength I needed to tell him, in our final session on my birthday.

◆

Going to Pieces

I looked at the clock as I stumbled out of bed. Only the clock wasn't in its place and I wasn't in my bed. I had fallen asleep on the couch. Slowly, the events of the night before washed over me. I had fallen asleep while waiting up for Lily. I had hoped to talk to her before I slept but I readjusted to the new reality—what better way to spend my birthday than to tell my daughter she had been involved in the accident that had killed the family of the man I liked, and then tell my patient who had been struggling with the loss of his family, that it was his intern who had been involved in the accident that had killed them. Nothing in my years of school and training had prepared me for such a dilemma.

◆

'Lily!' I screamed hoarsely, stumbling into the kitchen.

Perhaps I wasn't loud enough. The clock on the stove said it was 8.22 a.m. and there was no way she could have been asleep.

'Lily!' I screamed again, from the bottom of the steps. If I have a choice in the matter, I avoid those steps.

After giving it a minute, I crept up and barged into her room. She wasn't there and her bed didn't look like it had been slept in. I panicked, ran down the steps to find my cell phone, and punched in her number.

She picked up and, without waiting, started singing 'Happy Birthday to you! Happy Birthday...'

'Lily! Lily! Where are you?' I rasped.

She didn't apologize. 'Oh! I sent you a message, Mom. Didn't you read it?' She had decided to 'pull an all-nighter at the office' so she could be completely free on my birthday. In fact, she was going to come back home early in the afternoon to cook us a special celebratory dinner.

Oh well! I'm going to have to flip my plan around again. I had lost track of how many times I had done that already.

◆

Later that evening I was ready, with my hand on my holster, waiting for Sam to walk in. *It's going to be now or never.* I had promised myself it wouldn't be a repeat performance of our previous session. I needed to get everything out in the open—for everyone's sanity. I barely heard the knocking over the chainsaw buzzing between my ears.

'Come in,' I called out.

The knocking continued.

'Come on...in,' I said, in a sing-song voice, belying my state of mind.

The knocking persisted.

Who is it, dammit? I had to get up and get the door myself.

It was Sam! I had no sooner opened the door, than, from behind a bunch of colourful balloons, he began singing that all too familiar jingle that was beginning to jangle my nerves, 'Happy Birthday to you! Happy Birthday…'

The buzzing in my head had become louder and drowned out the rest of it. *How does he know? Must have been Lily!*

'Birthday girl, do I have a surprise for you? It's more a secret actually…well, both in a way.'

Ha! You think you have a surprise? Wait till you hear what I have to tell ya! It was almost a shame he couldn't read my mind.

'First, the secret—I deliberately scheduled this session because I knew it was your birthday.'

'Now get your umbrella and let's get going—for the surprise.'

I finally jolted myself. 'Sam, I have something to tell you.'

He had barged his way in and deposited the balloons in a corner of the room. 'Absolutely not! It can wait.'

'No, it can't,' I said as sternly as I could but it was challenging to maintain a commensurate expression while being distracted by the balloons pitching back and forth.

He must have gotten the hint, because his tone changed as well. 'Well, Cynthia, actually it must. You see—I have these tickets for a one-time talk at the Transit Museum. It's going to begin any minute now and I don't want us—no, strike that— you, to miss it.'

He was holding out two tickets to the talk I had wished I could have gone to with someone special!

He continued, 'And I have it on good authority that neither do you.' He winked.

He was already pushing me out the door, ever so deftly. I wondered whether he was getting away with it because I really wanted to go for the talk or because of my feelings for him. I added that to my growing list of imponderables. The talk must have been great, judging by the applause at the end of it. I, of course, didn't hear a thing. From the looks of it, he was distracted too—he kept looking over in my direction. Each time he asked if I was enjoying it, all I did was nod.

◆

When we stepped back out, the wind was howling and I wanted to join it. A summer storm was about to breach and there was heavy rain in the forecast for the night. *The entire universe but for two people seems to understand my turmoil!*

I pulled Sam back into the entrance of the museum and had to shout to be heard, 'We really have to talk now.'

'Oh, Cynthia,' he said with his hand to his heart, 'I'm so glad you liked the talk. You're most welcome!' And he burst out laughing.

If only a lightning bolt could strike down and... I didn't let myself finish the thought.

I was fuming. Apparently, he could tell. 'Okay! Okay! I'll tell you what—one of my favourite restaurants is right next door. Let's go grab a drink there and you can tell me everything that's on your mind.'

I was about to have a nervous breakdown. The last morsels of sanity, and those of resolve, fought back in unison. 'But I have plans with Lily.'

He was up to the challenge. 'Oh yeah, I know! We still have time till your next train and in the worst case I'll drop you home myself. I wouldn't want you to miss the treat she has in store for... Well, let me not say any more.' He had tilted his head and was smiling—possibly pleased with himself for knowing more than I did.

And just for that, I should invite him over for dinner—it

would serve him right to try her cooking!

'No, Sam! Right here,' I insisted.

'Okay! Let's do this—let's get to the station and we can talk there. That way, we can get out of this weather and make sure you get there in time.'

The words were the first reasonable utterances he had made all evening. We huddled together and walked out, braving the elements. We walked in silence for a few minutes and then, as we turned a corner, I realized he wasn't taking us to the station. He was taking us away from it.

I was about to scream bloody murder, when I heard a preemptive echo.

◆

Surprise

'Over here! Hurry!' Lily was screaming, waving for us to enter the restaurant as she held the door open. It wasn't the door to his favourite restaurant, unless his favourite restaurant happened to be the same as mine.

As we rushed into the safety of the foyer, they both yelled, 'Surprise!' and broke out into the tune that had turned into a haunting reminder of the spoof that was my birthday. Only, it wasn't as annoying as before. I was happier—I was with both of them—neither could ever know how much. I hadn't ever experienced such euphoric agony.

Sam had made reservations and Lily had been in on it all the time. If I remember correctly, her defence was, 'Even I know better than to cook for you!'

When the waiter came to take our drinks order, Lily was upset to find out the restaurant wouldn't serve her alcohol. 'Not even a teeny bit'—the waiter had echoed her words and laughed. She didn't find it amusing and had proceeded to dispense a stern sermon on European culture.

No sooner had the waiter left, than her demeanour changed.

She turned to me, 'How was it? Did you enjoy it?'

I had loved the idea of being there but the event had been a blur, so I faked it. 'Oh, absolutely!'

She bounced excitedly on her seat while looking at Sam. 'See, I told you! I knew she'd love it.'

I continued, 'You wouldn't believe—I had come across this event the other day and wanted to go so badly, but it was already sold out. Was it your idea?'

She dismissed my suggestion with a wave of her hand. 'Rubbish! It was completely his idea. I thought it was a good one but wasn't sure. The dinner was mine, and that's because I have an agenda.'

I felt the blood rush to my face. *What agenda does she have? Is she trying to set me up with Sam? I wouldn't put anything past her.*

I ignored her last comment, turned to Sam, and put my hand on his. 'Thank you! Really—it was the sweetest surprise ever. How'd you know I'd like it?'

He put his hand on mine. 'Given the number of books you have on Grand Central in your office, it doesn't take a locomotive engineer to figure it out. Although, I have to say, I was a little afraid…'

'Afraid for me? Oh, don't be silly,' I interrupted.

'No, no! Not afraid for you. Afraid of you! I was afraid you might know so much about its history that you might correct the speaker all the time or, worse yet, jump onto the stage and give the talk yourself. I would have left.'

Lily threw her head back and laughed. Sam was a little more tentative—it's what might have saved him from my wrath.

'Very funny,' I retorted. 'If I were you, I'd be afraid of me right about now!'

Lily's laugh got louder. Sam's sputtered to a stop.

'No, seriously—I'm glad you thought of it—I can't thank you enough,' I said.

'You can try—by not charging me for the session for one.'

'Now that is funny,' I said laughing. 'We'll just have to see who laughs their way to the bank, now won't we?' I raised my eyebrows mischievously.

He was not laughing at all—it was the desired effect.

The waiter brought us our drinks and took special pleasure in announcing Lily's 'might-as-well-be cranberry juice'. Lily wasn't amused but didn't say anything as Sam proposed a toast to their 'secret-ary'. They both laughed, to my dismay. I didn't want to be anyone's secret-bearer ever again. Awareness of my not-so-little yet not-so-guilty secrets came flooding back. I couldn't believe I had actually forgotten about them.

◆

Lily excused herself. I was sure she was going to go give the waiter another piece of her mind.

Sam turned to me, 'What did you want to talk about?'

'Huh?' I had forgotten again. *I must really be happy.*

'All evening you've been itching to talk to me about something and now "huh"? In fact, I was concerned it was why you looked so distracted during the talk. I was actually afraid you were upset.'

By then the waiter was setting our plates, but started rushing as Lily walked back to the table. He felt the need to explain he didn't want the 'young lady to say stuff' to him again, and I was sure Lily had settled the score.

There was no way I was going to ruin the moment for everyone, so I told him it could wait. He looked at me askance, as if to say he didn't really believe me. I guessed he understood women well.

The food was excellent. The dessert was great too—Sam had ordered a cake, which the staff brought out singing, ensuring that everyone was staring at me. The highlights, however, were the company, the conversation, and a strange, fleeting sense of family I was enjoying, yet felt I didn't deserve. While Lily couldn't drink and Sam wasn't drinking, I needed to—so I plied it on thick.

◆

As the meal came to an end, Lily announced, 'Before Mom passes out, I'd like to propose a toast too—to two of my "favouritest" people.'

Sam laughed. I was conscious enough to wonder if he had laughed at her alluding to my state of inebriation or at her having used his word. Neither scenario impressed me much.

Lily continued, 'And not only to my favourites, but also to two people who, in their own special ways, have helped me understand and find courage.'

'To courage,' she boomed, which was echoed by Sam and followed by the clink of our glasses. I mumbled unintelligibly, not because I couldn't enunciate, but because the word had lost all meaning.

She wasn't done. 'Also, before we leave, I have a gift for you, Mom…actually two.' She handed me two envelopes and asked me to open the one on top first. It contained two return-tickets to Spain. 'For us—all expenses paid,' she said, followed by raising both hands in the air and a 'Woohoo!'

Before I could even thank her, she prodded me to open the other one. It contained a piece of paper, which looked like an invoice or a receipt of some kind.

I wasn't sure what to make of it. *Is she asking me for money for the tickets or is she telling me she has already paid for them? Didn't she just say 'all expenses paid'?*

Either way, it didn't seem like a very exciting gift. 'Thank you?' I said, not intending for it to sound like a question.

'Take it out all the way, Mom, and look carefully,' she insisted.

And I did. And then it hit me. It was a receipt from NYU. *Has she decided to go to NYU?* I gasped. 'Is this what I think it is? You better not be shitting me, young lady!'

'Language, Mom!' she chided teasingly and they started laughing.

I could barely get the words out. 'Are you…sure? I mean…'

She put a hand on mine. 'Yes, Mom, I've talked to Sam about it as well—I'm gonna continue working part-time at his firm while going to school at NYU.'

While they both continued laughing, I broke into tears. 'You guys are mean! I need more alcohol.'

She got up and hugged me. 'Speaking of mean…I don't want to be mean to you, Sam, so I have a gift for you too.'

He sat up in his chair. 'Oh you do, do you? You are so full of surprises!' he said, rubbing his palms and flashing a million-dollar smile.

She was looking straight at him and her voice became softer. 'There was a reason I raised my glass to the two of you and to courage. I meant every word I said, but this process of discovery might not have started, had it not been for you.'

She spoke slowly, 'You've helped me be able to talk to Mom, and the result has been beautiful. She quoted you to encourage me to talk to my ex-boyfriend, and the result was… well…less beautiful but still positive. You also gave me the idea to confront the source of my secrets and fears.'

Her voice was almost hoarse. 'And that's what I did all day today. I found the place where something terrible may have happened quite some time back…and I may have been able to…help, but couldn't.'

I had no idea where she was going. Besides, I was elated about her decision to stay local.

'Even there, I discovered something beautiful,' She reached under the table, and Sam and I exchanged bewildered glances as I heard her unzipping her backpack.

She brought out a bunch of beautiful red and white flowers—the same ones Sam had brought for me—the ones he had planted for William at the site of the accident. 'I discovered these most beautiful flowers and I couldn't think of anyone better than you to give them to,' and she extended the bunch to him.

I froze. As far as I could tell, he froze too. I was sure my brain was about to flatline.

Had she not wanted to say something to me, she might have noticed his reaction, or rather the lack of it. She looked at me. 'You've seen them before, right Mom? They were on our counter when I came back from Spain, and I had asked you what they were called.'

By then Sam's fingers were curled around hers, which were still clutching the flowers. He was looking straight at the flowers.

'But you didn't know.' She turned to Sam. 'So…I spent the whole afternoon at the library trying to find out their name. And I did—just before I got here. They have the most unique name I've ever heard…'

◆

Sweet William

'Sweet William!' Sam and Lily said it at the same time. They were staring at each other. For me, it was too much and I broke down. I couldn't even begin to fathom what he must have been going through at the time.

Lily's eyes darted between the two of us before settling on me. 'Why are you crying? Mom? Are you okay?'

All I could do was shake my head.

She looked at Sam. By that time, his eyes were bloodshot too. He got up, went over to her, got down on his knees, and hugged her tightly.

'Mmph!' She let out a breath. She found my hand and clasped it firmly. 'Okay! I'm now officially freaked out. What is up with the two of you? You look like you've seen a ghost and she can't stop crying. What is it?'

'Nothing, Lily!' he said, not letting go of her. 'All of this is…so thoughtful of you… I think we both got overwhelmed.'

She tried looking at me over her shoulder but couldn't. I just squeezed her hand and kept shaking my head. It seemed like ages before Sam released her. When he did, she excused herself to go to the washroom. I was afraid she might be running away. And then I was just afraid, because I realized I was alone with Sam.

I looked at Sam sitting in Lily's chair and waited for a volcano to erupt. He stayed silent. And I couldn't speak.

He finally looked at me. 'Is this what you've been trying to talk to me about?'

I nodded between sobs. 'Mm…hmm… I just found out myself…and have really been trying… I'm so sorry…'

He put his hand on mine and looked into my eyes. 'No, please don't. No one else has helped me get through this more— so do whatever, but don't apologize. It's like you said—no one needs to be sorry.'

He looked over to where the washrooms were. I assumed he must have seen Lily returning. He spoke softly but rapidly. 'Just tell me this—were they responsible?'

There was so much I needed to say, but no clue how or where to begin. I spoke softly too. 'I don't think so. He was fooling around…but it was…a deer.'

By then, Lily was back. 'What? You two namby-pambies are still at it? Listen—I'm sorry for the gifts—remind me never to…'

Sam stopped her. 'Shush! We'll stop. It's okay.' He laughed. And so did Lily.

I didn't think I would ever laugh again. I had had a lot to eat and was full, but still felt hollow in the pit of my stomach.

Lily shot a glance at our hands and then looked at me. 'Phew! Mom, can we please get out of here now, or we'll miss the last train back home!'

He was still holding my hand. 'No way are you taking the train back. I'll drop you.'

She sat down in his chair. 'Really? Are you sure you can

drive through the tears? Big sissies, the two of you!'

Sam laughed again. 'Yeah, am sure.'

'But the weather ought to be really bad by now. How will you get back?' I asked. I was scared to disagree with him, but I was also afraid of not being alone with him. I just needed him to myself, so I could explain everything. *This is how people go crazy*, I thought.

'Don't worry about me—I'll be okay. Besides, my car is right outside,' he said.

I was going to resist, but he pressed my hand gently. I caved. I didn't have much more resistance to offer that evening.

His car was right outside indeed. *He obviously planned this to perfection!*

The weather was out of control—it was pouring pretty heavily. *A befitting climax to the evening!*

Once in the car, Sam and I were pretty quiet.

Lily, on the other hand, was still chirpy. 'Hey Sam, switch on the wipers, would you?'

He looked at her in the rear-view mirror, 'But they're already on.'

'No! I mean for your eyes.' She burst out laughing.

'Very funny!' and he joined her.

She waited for him to stop. 'What happened in there? You didn't like the flowers? I can get you new ones tomorrow. You like roses, or is it orchids? Just name it, mister!'

'Speaking of which, how'd you know what they're called?' She didn't wait for a response. 'If I'd known you're Mister Horticulture, I would have just asked you. It would have saved me a whole lot of time.'

'Stop it, Lily!' I tried to sound threatening but sounds barely escaped my lips. *If only she knew.*

She was having a merry time. 'And you? What happened to you? I can always take the tickets back and exchange them for flowers if you'd like, you know!'

'Or is it that you're having second thoughts about my decision to go to NYU? You were looking forward to some freedom, weren't you? Especially now that you've found… ahem… Bet that's what it is!' She whacked the back of my headrest. 'See, I'd love to oblige but I don't think you're all grown up and ready to be by yourself just yet.'

Sam was laughing heartily by then. I joined in, more because I needed to camouflage my cheeks. I wasn't sure what she had meant by 'now that you've found' but I was sure glad she hadn't finished the thought.

Then, Sam opened up as well. 'When do you think you'll go to Spain? Before college, I assume.'

Lily clapped her hands in delight. 'Depends on when I can get off work. I wonder who I need to cosy up to…to apply for an extended vacation… Hmm…'

He glanced at her in the mirror. 'Ah ha! We'll just have to see about that, now, won't we?'

She stopped bouncing. 'No! Please no! I'll be nice to you. I promise—no more mean jokes and apparently no more flowers too! Okay, okay! That was the last one, I promise.'

He laughed, and it sounded carefree. Things seemed to have gone back to normal, but I wasn't convinced if Sam's behaviour wasn't an affectation for Lily's benefit.

◆

Acceptance

It was pouring heavily and traffic was slow. Sam was focused on the road and we'd been driving in silence for a while. Suddenly, he slapped his forehead and laughed. 'I'm sorry! I'm so scattered—I'm so used to driving to my place that I completely forgot.'

I realized we had driven to Westchester instead—in fact, I could already see his house in the distance. Lily and I shrieked over each other. In a matter of seconds, we were pulling into his driveway. She and I started laughing too. In my case, it was more out of nervousness than amusement.

Before either of us could utter a word, Sam mumbled, 'Well, let's get out of this weather at least,' and stepped out of the car. When we were safely inside, he said, 'You know what—now that we're here and the weather out is crazy, why don't you both take the guest room? You'll find everything you need there. It's a holiday tomorrow—I'll drive you home first thing in the morning.'

'Besides,' he continued, 'I didn't drink because I knew I had to drive back and god knows I could use one right now.'

Personally, another drink would have bordered on abuse, but I thought a hangover would be a good remedy for my state of mind. 'Bring it on!' I waved.

Lily chimed in. 'Yeah, Mom was drinking enough for all three of us. Hey, wait a minute! This way, I can have a glass too—you wouldn't mind, now would you, Boss?' She was batting her eyelids furiously and flashing him her best smile.

He laughed. 'Of course not! What better way to get a vacation approved than to have a drink with the boss?' He winked at her.

I joined in the banter in spite of myself. 'Laugh all you want, Sam, but I wonder what it says about your capacity—if in spite of being sober, we ended up in the wrong county!'

We laughed, he poured us wine, and the matter of where we'd spend the night was considered settled.

Lily raised her glass and proposed her second toast of the evening. 'To laughing!' she said, 'And to no more crying—you girls, please!'

We were laughing, drinking, and chatting for a long time till Lily lay down on the couch.

As soon as she closed her eyes, I turned to Sam, 'I want to explain... I really...'

He covered my mouth with his hand. 'No, really! There is nothing to explain. I've been connecting the dots and think I've figured it out. They're just kids and it must have taken a lot of courage for him to go to the police. If he was really at fault, he wouldn't have done that.'

I took his hand away from my mouth and held it.

He continued after a brief pause. 'There's nothing good that can come out of any explanations...for anyone. Besides, nothing anyone can do will ever bring them back...'

I continued gazing at our hands. 'That's a very mature way of looking at it. You sound almost happy…'

He interrupted me. 'Yes! I'm happy. I'm finally happy.'

Lily stirred, so he continued in a softer voice, 'Why? Aren't you happy that I'm happy? Isn't that what you've been working so hard for all this time?'

I felt the need to defend myself. 'No, no! That's not what I meant.'

He, too, looked down at our hands before continuing. 'You've helped me confront and make peace with my relationship—something I couldn't do even while I was in it. I'm glad I had Will for almost thirteen years—I tried to make them the best I could for him. I wish I could have given him the rest of my years, but sadly I can't. The most important thing is that I'm at peace. It's not like the pain has gone, but there's a lot to look forward to as well.' He looked into my eyes. 'I have the two of you in my life…in a way…I couldn't have possibly planned.'

For a brief moment, I forgot about my guilt. I felt happy for him and that my work was done. I put my head on his shoulder. I wanted to tell him how I felt about him but couldn't bring myself to. Still, I could have let the moment last for eternity. When I straightened up, he stood up and left the room.

I got up too, walked to the glass-wall overlooking the yard, and stood there watching the rain fall.

He brought back a sheet and tucked Lily under it. I smiled at him. And then, without taking his eyes off me, he walked slowly over to my side.

Something about the moment made me buckle. 'Sam… There's something else I need to tell you.'

Lily rolled over, cocooning herself tighter under the covers. We looked at her. Sam turned his gaze back at me, 'I don't think you need to.' His hand fell by the side of mine, and our fingers slowly intertwined.

As I turned into him, I saw a pale car pull into the neighbour's driveway. A second later, I had forgotten everything as I was way too deep into him.

We let a few moments pass before he led me through the living room and switched off the lights on our way up. As we ascended the floating staircase hand in hand, he said, 'This is pretty crazy... You said it was okay... I don't need to be sorry, right?'

I laughed. 'Yes, it is...and no, you needn't be.'

◆

ACCEPTANCE

Friends, Finally

The next morning I woke up feeling wonderful. Opening my eyes, I saw he was still asleep as blissfully—I hoped—as I had just been. He was right. It had been crazy…much more than okay…perfect in fact; and nothing either one of us needed to be sorry about. I continued looking at him for a while, taking in his features. I looked at his scar—thought of running a finger on it but decided against it. I wondered how he got it. I thought about all the other things I didn't know about him and hoped to start finding out soon.

◆

I slipped out of bed slowly, so as not to disturb him. My thoughts wandered to Lily and I made my way downstairs. The couch was empty, except for the sheet that had been neatly folded. I heard what I thought was the clank of a cup against the counter. I made my way to the kitchen.

Sure enough, she was sitting with her back to me, drinking coffee and looking outside at the newly washed world.

I sneaked up behind her and gave her a kiss on the back

of her head—something I could do consistently without risk of injury. I began pouring myself a cup of coffee, without making eye contact.

'Ahem! Ahem!' She cleared her throat about half a dozen times.

I kept looking into my cup and asked, 'Something wrong with your throat, dear?'

'Not at all, Mom.'

'Slept well?' I asked, stealing a quick glance at her.

Her gaze continued to sear. 'Yes, very well! And so did you I'm sure... Hehehe!'

'What does that mean? What's so funny?' I still wasn't looking at her.

'Nothing. Nothing at all. It's a perfectly comfortable house and I'm sure you slept really well...in the guest room. Could you tell me where it is, please? I'd love to see it.' She continued giggling.

I had to put an end to her shameless shenanigans. 'Breakfast? What would you like to have?' I banged the coffee cup on the counter, intending for it to serve as an appropriate punctuation.

She just laughed over it. 'Where's Sam?'

'Still slee...eeping... I guess.' I had to course-correct to avoid her trap, but blood had already rushed to my face.

We both looked at each other and started laughing.

'Relax, Ma! I'm not a baby. It's not like I need to learn about the birds and the bees. So what does this mean?' Her eyes were round like saucers.

I looked away. *It's way too early for this conversation.* I burrowed my head in the fridge. 'Let me get breakfast started. Eggs okay?'

She persisted. 'C'mon, Mom! I mean, are you both...'

'Lily!' I screeched, opened a few cabinets, and started taking out pots and pans loudly in order to drown her voice. My eyes fell on a beautiful little detail that I regretted having missed on the night of his birthday. Each cabinet pull was a tiny, colourful replica of Gaudí's dragon. I ran my fingertips on its tiles and it reminded me of a niggle from the past. Clearly, he knew more about Gaudí than I had credited him with. I was surprised he hadn't said anything about the dragon embossed on my notebook—it had been staring him in the face for more than a year. *What other secrets might he be keeping?*

I could neither revel in my discovery nor focus on my thoughts as Lily kept going. I needed a different strategy to shut her up. I walked up to where Sam had left the flowers the night before. They reminded me of all that she didn't know. I met her eyes squarely. 'We are not having this conversation right now, Lily, and besides, there's a whole lot you don't know.'

She didn't back down. 'I know all I need to know. I know that he likes you and I know that you two…'

I interrupted her. 'I'm really not listening to this right now.' I grabbed the flowers and continued walking towards a vase kept on a small table at the corner of the glass and brick walls.

'Okay, okay! We won't talk about the two of you. Can we talk about me?'

'Sure!' I smiled, as I shot back over my shoulder, 'That's my "favouritest" topic, hon!'

My mind wandered to the day when Sam and Lily had first met—how his knowledge of the store, Hot Topic, had ignited their connection. I'm sure it was just a coincidence—one I was supremely thankful for. To me, life itself is a string of coincidences and, to be perfectly honest, I don't get our obsession with either controlling or explaining them. I skipped over the thought as I became aware that a part of me was disappointed the friendly joust with Lily had come to an end—it was the part of me that was thrilled to have Lily in my life as a friend, finally.

I was at the glass wall and wiped some of the condensation off it. The last few days had been somewhat of a roller coaster. My world had been twirling rapidly and I had been struggling to focus. The last time I felt that way was in the first session with Sam, almost a year and a half back. At that moment however, looking out, I felt I could see everything more clearly.

◆

Only Not

Not only could I see everything more clearly, but I also had a wider view, including one into the neighbour's property. I saw the same pale car from the night before, reversing. As it appeared from behind the hedges separating the driveways, I realized it wasn't pale—I had seen the white trunk of a police car. *I didn't know Sam's neighbour was in the police.* I let out a shriek as I saw the car backing into a rather large branch which must have fallen during the storm.

'You okay, Mom?' Lily asked.

The driver must have noticed the branch too—I saw the car stop and the door on the driver's side opening. The driver walked away to inspect the branch. He was walking with a limp. My eyes hovered over him and focused on a small wooden shed at the far end of the yard. I noticed a few old and rusty bicycles in it. It occurred to me that the driver must be none other than John—Sam's cycling buddy—the one he had gone on vacation with. My deduction fit—I remembered Sam mentioning John was a neighbour and that he had injured his leg badly in a fall.

I picked up the vase and walked back to the sink to fill it with water. I looked over at Lily. 'I'm sorry. You were saying?'

She took a sip of her coffee. 'Seeing you with Sam made me think of Roy. Now, don't worry—I'm not thinking of getting back together with him or anything crazy like that. I don't think I told you the other day—he went to the police.'

I had to bite my tongue to stop myself from saying I knew. It hit me again—I still needed to break it to her and I hadn't said anything to Sam about her not knowing, either.

She continued. 'It was pretty brave of him, Mom. He talked to his mother and they went straight to the sheriff and told him everything.'

Everything? I reduced the flow of water to a trickle. I wondered if it was the right time and place to tell her everything too. I did feel relieved—I felt the worst was over.

She put her cup down. 'I asked him for details but he didn't want to talk about it.'

I turned the faucet off and looked back at her. That would be the opening I needed. But Lily wasn't done. 'He said what's important is that the police had decided not to press any charges… Anyway, the sheriff was very nice and understanding but had insisted Roy get counselling. And that's what I want to talk to you about.'

'Huh?' All of a sudden, I wasn't sure where she was going. I leaned back against the sink with the vase in one hand.

'When I met him the other day, it was clear that counselling has really helped him. He's been doing well and has been sober ever since…so…I was thinking…I'm not totally closed to the idea anymore.'

I had to blink and shake my head to refocus. 'Really? Are you saying what I think you are?'

She was smiling. 'Yeah! We can try and see if it works for us. No harm I guess.'

'You have no idea how happy that makes me… Mmmuaah!' I planted another kiss on her head—I couldn't get enough of it.

Lily reciprocated by blowing a kiss in the air. 'Cool! And you know the best part—he went to the sheriff a few weeks after the incident.'

I had just about started walking away, but I stopped. 'Sorry… What?' I managed a whisper.

She must have heard me. 'Yeah, he went by himself. I mean, with his mother of course.'

'No! When you said incident, you meant after you went and spoke with him, right?'

'No, Mom! I meant right after the accident—much before we spoke. That's what he had been trying to tell me at school…'

I stopped listening to her. The all-too-familiar buzzing in my head started again. I slowly started walking towards the dining table. Over the sound of the buzzing, I was trying to figure out the significance of Roy's dates. I tried to remember if Sam had actually answered my question about when Roy had gone to the police. He hadn't. 'Why does that matter?' is what he had said.

It mattered to me. It mattered then. Immensely. The dates were far from lining up with when Sam had told me about 'Rob…or Ron…or something like that'. My mind raced, salvaging snippets of memories from the past eighteen months. I recalled Sam's nightmares of a woman's voice telling him she knew something. I remembered him figuring out Lily ought to be in college and asking if she was travelling with her boyfriend. It struck me that when he had dropped me home for the first time, he had reassured me it wasn't a detour even before I gave him my address.

I thought of the dragon on my notebook and on Sam's cabinets—they reminded me of my niggles about him having known of Gaudí all along but not having mentioned it even once. My mind went back to Roy's dates. They were still not lining up, but other things were—unsettlingly so. Even though I believe everything is just a coincidence, those were far too many and they were all pointing in the same direction—*Sam knew more than he had let on. How much did he know?*

I thought of Sam's anger when he first came in and remembered James's question about what the anger was directed at. The realization that Sam's anger had not been directed at the situation but rather at me, struck with blinding clarity. *Even if he knew everything when he first came in, how could he have known?*

I was almost at the corner table but had stopped dead in my tracks. Suddenly, everything began shaking violently—even though I was standing very, very still. I sensed my grip loosening around the vase but I couldn't do anything about it.

I saw John had managed to remove the branch and was limping back towards the car. He was wearing his police uniform and had paused by the trunk of the car to put his jacket back on. As he did, I could see him more clearly. There was something familiar about him but I couldn't place it. *I haven't met John, now have I? Perhaps at Sam's birthday party…*

And then it hit me. If it was John, it wasn't just John's face. It was also the face of Sheriff Matthews.

Could it be that Sam's neighbour was Sheriff…John…fucking… Matthews?! It was one thing to have known Lily's name, but how had he known what she looked like, the night of the party? Watching him limp back to the front of his car, my thoughts raced to the last thing he had said that night—something about him not being able to run after Sam. After all, we had just stood in one spot the whole time he had been there, and I hadn't seen him walk in either.

ONLY NOT

I heard a noise upstairs—it sounded like Sam moving about. I remembered how every time Sam talked about John, he was conveniently reminded of the sheriff. It struck me that Sam had known the 911-call was from a gas station all along, but had only mentioned it was from a public telephone the first time he had brought it up. *If Sheriff Matthews and John are the same person and if John is Sam's cycling buddy, it all adds up!*

In that instant I realized how mistaken I was. I had been thinking Sam was the one with the unanswered questions and I the one with the secrets, but everything had just turned inside out. If Sam and the sheriff were close friends, that explained how Sam would have known everything. More eerily, it was apparent that he knew everything from the very beginning, from our very first call.

The buzzing between my ears was unbearably loud by then, but the condensation from the glass wall had all but disappeared. I could see everything, crystal clear. The only thing I wasn't sure about was why. *Why hadn't he come clean?*

All of Sam's comments that he was doing something crazy flooded my mind. Then his last words from the night before ricocheted in my head—'This is pretty crazy…I don't need to be sorry, right?'

I felt the vase slip from my fingers.

Lily's scream pierced through the loud buzzing—she must have seen the vase slip. The vase was not the only thing that crashed around me.

I remembered how Sam had described the site of the accident, 'Glass everywhere…millions of shards…almost like stars…only not.'

I just stood there with my mouth open, one hand clenched in a fist, and the other around the Sweet Williams.

Acknowledgements

To acknowledge everyone who has elevated me would be akin to writing a memoir. So, to those whom I may have inadvertently omitted, do remember that 'to forget is human, to forgive divine'.

Dad, my guinea-reader, who ironically seems to have stopped reading since having read the first seventeen versions of the manuscript. I try, every Tuesday, not to ask why.

Mom, for providing fuel in more ways than I can count and foregoing her favourite television shows to read the manuscript in one sitting.

Mukul Sahgal and Shreya Chakraborti, for seeing potential and trusting I could do better; Fauzia Burke for sagely advice and spurring me on; Christopher Skinner, my serendipitous partner-in-crime, for the second-most fun part of this journey.

Kapish Mehra for his time and wisdom; Elina Majumdar for her sincere and diligent editing; Vasundhara Raj Baigra, Gaurav Sethi, and Shivendra Singh at Rupa Publications for their tireless efforts to bolster the quality of every aspect of my debut effort.

Nirmala Tandon, Sandeep Kapur, and Rema Harish at IIMPACT for their enthusiasm and support for my project, even though it may only be a drop in their ocean.

Puneet Gulati, Sanjeev Khanna, Puneet Wadhwa, and Shalini Kala at store-partner Barista India for their inventiveness, camaraderie, and energy that is bringing so much positivity to planning for the launch.

Abhishek and Tanushree Gandhi, Shobhit Kumar, and Aleem Uddin Siddiqui for whom helping me was gratification enough.

Amrita Varma, who worked sleeplessly to help me connect with my ultimate personal goal—that of empathizing with my characters and readers.

Most importantly, you, the reader for taking a leap of faith and sharing your feedback. Yes, I would love to hear from you!

Drop me a note at www.neelmullick.com.

◆

Read4Charity

Neel Mullick firmly believes that improving the state of children's education holds the best hope of bringing about a future brighter than the one we currently seem to be hurtling towards. The author will be donating half of his royalties earned from *Dark Blossom* to IIMPACT, an NGO with the aim of breaking the cycle of illiteracy that plagues young girls from socially and economically impoverished communities. IIMPACT currently educates 50,000 girls in 1,500 Indian villages.

Neel Mullick decided to work with IIMPACT after personally visiting many centres and convincing himself that their unequivocal focus in channelling 100 per cent of donor funds towards their mission and clear delivery model relying on local community-based learning centres, are precisely the need of the hour.

◆

WinTrip2NY

The author has created an experiential competition for the readers of *Dark Blossom*. Up for grabs are business and economy class return tickets to NYC (or destination of choice) and an iPad Mini 4.

All readers have to do is sign up at www.WinTrip2NY.com, read the book, and articulate their opinion on just one aspect of the story.

Akin to our own lives, discovering the characters' personalities and motivations is an ongoing journey. The author is hopeful of having the company and opinions of insightful readers along for the rest of it.

All details and rules of the competition can be found at www.WinTrip2NY.com.

◆